# PRAISE FOR:

# MON DIEU, LOVE

Love takes many forms in Jane Blunschi's *"Mon Dieu, Love"*—of a mother, of sisters and their lovers; the kind of love that saves us, the kind that brings us to the brink of ruin, the kind we want and the kind we deserve, and the love of those who help us to know the difference. What a captivating first book.

—Lacy M. Johnson, author of
*More City Than Water*

The patron saint of lesbian angst, Jane V. Blunschi's *Mon Dieu, Love* is a catalogue of queer domesticities. Think *Tender Buttons,* but contemporary characters: southern, and messy. Blunschi crafts prayers from rage, from tenderness, from addiction—a rosary in which every other bead is a love letter to never knowing the answer. The not knowing doesn't keep these stories from asking. "But doesn't ecstasy stay in your spinal cord, in the fluid?" "What should I call you?" "What else could she bear to hear?" Blunschi's debut is a bruise that feels good to touch.

—Canese Jarboe, author of
*Dark Acre*

Jane V. Blunschi crafts stories that blend humor and empathy. Her prose displays a sensitivity to her characters, inviting readers to appreciate their flaws in the same ways one might appreciate the flaws of close friends or family members. I read this novella in one sitting; once invited into these characters' worlds, it was difficult to leave. Blunschi clearly is an author the world should watch.

—Lindsay A. Chudzik, Editor in Chief
of Feels Blind Literary

Jane V. Blunschi's *Mon Dieu, Love* is a novel of queer love and entanglement that astonishes with its capacity to both disturb and endear. Inside a world, where characters make ethically dubious choices, somewhat repeatedly, I find myself rooting for their recoveries and willing them to reconfigure their dreams for the future. It is a surprising, sometimes uncomfortable, often funny, deeply nuanced journey that binds your attention until its end. A magnetic debut.

—Renee Gladman, author of
the Ravicka novel cycle

# MON DIEU, LOVE

# WINNER OF THE 2022 CLAY REYNOLDS NOVELLA PRIZE

## Jane V. Blunschi, *Mon Dieu, Love*
### Selected by Renee Gladman

*Established in 2001, The Clay Reynolds Novella Prize highlights one book a year that excels in the novella format.*

## PREVIOUS WINNERS INCLUDE:

Deirdre Danklin, *Catastrophe*
Selected by Leslie Jill Patterson

Cecilia Pinto, *Imagine the Dog*
Selected by Hannah Pittard

Dylan Fisher, *The Loneliest Band in France*
Selected by Rita Bullwinkel

Patrick Stockwell, *The Light Here Changes Everything*
Selected by Clay Reynolds

The complete list of winners can be found on our website:
texasreviewpress.org

# MON DIEU, LOVE

*a novella*

## JANE V. BLUNSCHI

TRP: The University Press of SHSU
Huntsville, Texas 77341

Library of Congress Cataloging-in-Publication Data
Names: Blunschi, Jane V., author.
Title: Mon dieu, love : a novella / Jane V. Blunschi.
Description: First edition. | Huntsville : TRP: The University Press
    of SHSU, [2023]
Identifiers: LCCN 2022048677 (print) | LCCN 2022048678 (ebook)
    | ISBN 9781680033434 (paperback) | ISBN 9781680033441 (ebook)
Subjects: LCSH: Sisters—Louisiana—Baton Rouge—Fiction. |
    Interpersonal relations—Fiction. | Baton Rouge (La.)—Fiction.
    LCGFT: Lesbian fiction. | Novellas.
Classification: LCC PS3602.L884 M66 2023 (print) | LCC PS3602.
    L884 | (ebook) | DDC 813/.6—dc23/eng/20221017
LC record available at https://lccn.loc.gov/2022048677LC ebook
record available at https://lccn.loc.gov/2022048678
FIRST EDITION
Author photo courtesy: Blunschi
Cover & interior design: PJ Carlisle
Printed and bound in the United States of America
First Edition Copyright: 2023
TRP: The University Press of SHSU
Huntsville, Texas 77341
texasreviewpress.org

# CONTENTS

I. Anger Prayer . . . . . . . . . . . . . . . . . . . . 1

II. Michael . . . . . . . . . . . . . . . . . . . . 10

III. Everybody Gets a Little Crush
Sometimes . . . . . . . . . . . . . . . . . . . . . 22

IV. Mind Me . . . . . . . . . . . . . . . . . . 30

V. Mon Dieu, Love . . . . . . . . . . . . . . 41

VI. The Apartment Song . . . . . . . 52

VII.  The Religious Life . . . . . . . 56

VIII. Cardio Annihilation . . . . 67

IX.  Hand to Mouth . . . . . . . . . 76

X. Thanks, Biscuit . . . . . . . . . . 84

XI.  All the Apps Again . . . . . . 93

XII.  Back In the Cup . . . . . . . . 105

Acknowledgments . . . . . . . . . . 109

# 1

## ANGER PRAYER

When Carrie left her wife, Whole Foods Market became a panacea for her grief. More than the expensive healthy groceries, she was drawn to the atmosphere of the store. Unlike shopping at the other health food store in town, a co-op that smelled like soy sauce and hot tempeh, shopping at Whole Foods made her feel as if taking care of herself could be creative and cute. It felt abundant.

"I could stand in front of that refrigerator full of kombucha all afternoon," she'd told Ashley, her doctor, during one of their weekly sessions.

Ashley nodded, made a note on the legal pad in her lap, and asked, "Has your stomach been bothering you? Are you drinking the kombucha for that?"

"It's not about the kombucha. I don't buy it. I just like to look."

Carrie wanted the divorce and was happy to no longer be married. She'd discovered that her wife Kim had been conducting a year-long affair with a woman who lived in Denver, a city Kim regularly visited for work. Carrie made this discovery in the most mundane and insulting of ways: the woman sent her a text message using Kim's phone. When the pic came in (from Kim she thought at first) Carrie didn't understand what she was seeing: An image of her wife standing topless in front of a mirror with a thick white towel wrapped around her waist and a toothbrush stuck in her mouth. Standing behind Kim, with her chin hooked over Kim's shoulder, was a stranger—was the woman who'd sent the text. One arm snaked around Kim's torso, her hand cupping Kim's breast. The other held Kim's phone, taking the picture; Carrie recognized the New Orleans Saints fleur-de-lis logo in gold on the case.

The woman included her phone number in the text.

> Call me. I want to talk to you about your wife.

Carrie did call, and she learned that Kim had recently ended her relationship with the woman, citing the culmination of her project in Denver as a convenient time for them to call it quits. This enraged the woman enough to text Carrie the picture and to inform her, during their ensuing phone conversation, that Kim had done the same thing to other women in Seattle, New Orleans, Santa Fe, and Dallas.

"Dallas really stings," Carrie told her mother, whose house she'd moved into temporarily. "I feel like every woman in Texas is exceptionally beautiful."

Still, her marriage had been unsatisfying for years in other mundane and insulting ways; petty fights about money, mediocre sex, and long, icy silences had replaced the friendship and attraction she and Kim had shared when they'd met a decade earlier.

To cope with her feelings, Carrie tried: therapy, Pilates, casual sex, and shopping for clothes, a habit that had begun to eat away at the settlement Kim agreed to. Carrie walked away from their eight-year marriage with enough for a down payment on a new house and a little bit of extra cash to play with—plus fifty-fifty custody of their yellow Lab, Christopher.

"Don't eat that money, Carrie," her mother warned. "Don't twenty-five dollar it away on trash."

"It's for cashmere sweaters," Carrie snapped, "not food."

She *was* eating the money, though. She'd begun to go to Whole Foods almost every day for one or two things—despite the fact that her mother kept the kitchen stocked with her favorite foods and cooked for the two of them every day—a white peach, a little tray of deviled eggs, a couple of stuffed grape leaves from the salad bar to hold her until supper time. She told herself that this was a very European way to shop, only buying what she'd need for that day, but she was not European. She lived in Baton Rouge.

The intensity of her sadness peaked on Friday nights. She hadn't quite gotten used to sleeping alone, so she made a fortress of long pillows beside her body to approximate Kim's body and snuggled up, throwing her arm and leg over the whole thing. One sleepless night she downed a couple of Benadryl, and as they worked their magic and she felt herself drifting off she kissed the pillow and ran her hand down the length of it whispering, "Sleep tight, baby. I love you."

Doing this was comforting and at the same time deeply embarrassing. To Carrie, it seemed like something a straight woman in a movie would do to deal with her loneliness.

The next night, after she brushed her hair and her teeth and put lotion on her face and hands and feet, she stared into her own eyes in the bathroom mirror and said, "No one is coming to kiss you goodnight. No one is going to hold you all night long." She swatted the extra pillows off Kim's side of the bed, slid under the covers and cried until she fell asleep.

For her codependency and grief, Ashley suggested that Carrie go to back Al-Anon. "Are you still doing your meetings?

Carrie took off her glasses and rubbed her eyes. "Yes, Doctor Ashley. I am still listening to people swallow coffee at Al-Anon." Carrie hated the sound of people chewing and swallowing, and was sometimes unnerved during Al-Anon meetings, where it seemed like everyone was slurping and swallowing coffee, even at six or seven o'clock in the evening. "Those people have an unquenchable thirst for coffee. I don't understand it. There should be a support group for that."

"Those people are *your* people, Carrie. You probably have more in common with them than you think. And please, call me Ashley. You can drop the 'doctor.'"

Carrie knew she belonged in Al-Anon; her initial anger toward Kim had softened too quickly to ambivalence, and Kim had already become one of the people Carrie was having casual sex with, which made her feel like a chump, and then she was furious all over again. She was comforted by the stories people told in the meetings about detachment, healing, and finding relief.

"I'm still trying to get some of that relief they keep talking about," she said to Ashley. "I started saying the Anger Prayer."

Carrie had learned about the Anger Prayer during a particularly rough phone call with her Al-Anon sponsor, Julie, a professor of history in her sixties who counted all eight of her grown children and her husband, a fellow professor who was long dead from heroin addiction, as her qualifiers—Judge Julie, people in the program called her—because of her tough love advice.

"Listen to me, Miss," Judge Julie scolded, "if you want to change, you have to surrender. Ask God to help you."

"Higher Power," Carrie corrected. "I don't say that word, Julie. I don't like it."

"Higher Power, then, H.P., whatever."

Julie sent Carrie a link to the prayer, a paragraph-long section of a book used by another twelve-step group.

> Say this every day for two weeks and see if it doesn't help . . .

she wrote, adding the smiley face with nerdy glasses emoji, followed by praying hands, pink heart, and for some reason, vanilla ice cream cone.

Carrie glanced over the prayer, but she felt raw after the

phone call. She drove to Whole Foods for a kombucha (finally) and a slice of pizza. Grief made her hungry.

Carrie liked to put on headphones and walk around Whole Foods, pretending her life was a movie. *Graceland* by Paul Simon was her ultimate breakup album, followed by *Damn the Torpedoes* and *Hounds of Love.* While she walked through the aisles, she pretended her life was a movie about a middle-aged lesbian who finally learns how to cook and is really really good at it, but doesn't understand what all the fuss is about when people take a bite of her food and close their eyes and swoon. At a potluck dinner party, she meets a sexy, grounded butch who just happens to be in therapy and who flips out over her crawfish étouffée or hummingbird cake or whatever, and they fall together in an ecstatic love that makes everyone they know jealous. Other couples secretly and not so secretly want what they have and pull them aside at every future potluck dinner party like, "I want what you two have." And her new girlfriend can't even *see* other women, much less embark on a series of sporadic, regionally determined affairs, because she is so in love with Carrie.

Carrie was standing in the check-out line at Whole Foods, sucking on a sample cup of organic coconut yogurt. The woman who was ringing up her groceries gave her a big bright smile as she placed her pizza and kombucha on the conveyor belt, along with a liter of Dr. Bronner's peppermint soap, a package of gluten-free crackers, and a nine-dollar box of green tea that she had not planned to buy.

"Your wife was just here," the woman chirped. Her name tag said Rachel. "She bought one of these," Rachel picked up the bottle of soap, waving it in Carrie's direction "in case you want to put it back."

Carrie froze. She had seen Kim at Whole Foods before, including one time soon after their divorce was finalized. They'd stopped to say hello because to ignore one another would have been ridiculous, and they ended up intensely kissing in the baking aisle, in front of the bottles of honey and agave nectar.

"I mean, unless you want to stock up," Rachel continued. "Nothing wrong with having a spare on hand."

"We're not married anymore." Carrie dug through her wallet, fumbling with a wad of tens and fives and finally sliding out a credit card to cover the bill.

"Oh, no. You broke up?"

Carrie looked squarely at Rachel. "We didn't break up. We got a divorce." A line was forming, and she could feel the eyes of the guy bagging groceries at the end of the belt on her face. Rachel's mouth made a perfect "O" of surprise, and then crumpled into an expression of pity, "Are you okay? Was it," Rachel lowered her voice and leaned over, "amicable?"

Carrie went blind. She tried to refocus on the enamel pins that covered Rachel's vest: a peach; a stylized version of Trixie Mattell's head with a thought bubble that said, *OH HONEY;* and a bisexual pride flag. "I'm sorry?" Carrie said.

Rachel doubled down, oblivious. "Are y'all cool? Are you still friends?"

"I can't talk about this. I'm sorry." Carrie snatched her credit card out of the reader and jammed it into her open wallet. "Actually, I'm not sorry. It's not your business, and I shouldn't have said anything at all."

Rachel reached for Carrie's wrist, "Oh, hey, I didn't mean—"

Carrie grabbed the handles of the brown paper grocery bag. "It's not your business. Just give me my groceries, please." She stalked out of the store, burning.

Carrie got into her car and drove to the edge of the parking lot, away from the light of the store's sign, where no other cars were parked. She opened the bottle of kombucha and took a couple of hard pulls, and then reached in the bag for the cardboard container holding her slice of pizza. She flipped it open and picked off every slice of pepperoni. She wadded those up and shoved them into her mouth, then ripped the entire slice in half, ignoring the black olives that bounced off her jeans into the space between her seat and the console. She folded one of the halves and pinched it closed, then tore it into even smaller pieces that she swallowed without chewing or tasting. When she'd finished the entire slice, she downed the rest of the kombucha and found the text from Julie with the Anger Prayer. She read it silently. The words that stood out to her: "God, save me from anger." She read it out loud, holding an image of Rachel-the-checkout-girl's face in her mind, and then an image of Kim's face in her mind, and then images of what Kim's women in Seattle, New Orleans, Santa Fe, and Dallas might look like in her mind. She gave the woman in Dallas a cluster of hormonal acne around her jawline. *God, save me,* she thought.

The Anger Prayer was a plea to a person's Higher Power to help them see that someone who continually pissed them off or hurt them was suffering from a spiritual sickness, and to motivate them to treat that person the way they'd treat a close friend who was sick.

"I avoid people when they're sick," she'd complained to Julie.

"You have a long way to go, Carrie. Next time, try asking what you can do for them first, and then run off."

The words "God, save me" became a sort of mantra that she allowed to run through her mind on a loop, blurring into a single word. *Godsaveme.* She wanted to change. Two weeks passed, and then two more, and Carrie felt the same. She stayed away from Whole Foods and invented reasons to zap Kim and drive her crazy. "I can't find the title for my car." *Godsaveme.* Social Security card. *Godsaveme.* She'd left a yoga mat in the closet of their guest bedroom. *Godsaveme.* Christopher was scratching more than usual; had Kim given the groomer his special shampoos? *Godsaveme.* His Prozac? *Godsaveme.* Did Kim have her copy of *Slow Lightning? Godsaveme.* Her copy of *Linda Goodman's Sun Signs? Godsaveme.* Her copy of *Love in the Time of Cholera? Godsaveme.* The diffuser for her blow dryer? *Godsaveme. Godsaveme. Godsaveme.* Even as she texted and called Kim, Carrie kept repeating the prayer and telling herself and her Higher Power that she wanted the Anger Prayer to work.

One Friday evening after work, she gave in and went back to

Whole Foods. She was craving a kombucha and wanted to treat herself, finally, to an expensive bottle of probiotics, the one that advertised fifty billion live cultures. As she pulled into a parking spot near the door, she noticed Kim's navy Outback parked two rows away. She knew it was Kim's car because Christopher was sitting in the front passenger seat. As she walked over to the car, she remembered the last conversation she'd had with Kim about Christopher. "He's scratching because he gets overheated," she'd explained. "He's too old to be outside hiking with you for an entire afternoon." Christopher was eleven.

"I know how to take care of him, Carrie. Back off."

"He's too old."

"When he's with you, he can stay indoors as much as you want." Kim said all of this in the same reasonable, measured tone she used to answer Carrie's many, many other requests, and this made Carrie angrier than ever.

She estimated that the temperature that evening had dropped into the seventies as the sun went down. It was still too hot for an elderly dog to hang out in a car while one of his owners took her time buying expensive snacks she'd probably pack into an airline-approved carry-on to later eat in bed with a woman whose time she hadn't wasted for eight years yet, Carrie thought. *Godsaveme.*

"Christopher, Christopher, Christopher," she called. Hearing his name, he snapped to attention, pushing his snout through the crack Kim had left in the window. *Saveme.* She ducked a little as she approached the door, even though she knew that Kim couldn't see her from inside, and then she straightened up and tried to act as if she were walking to her own car, so that the other people leaving the store with their TGIF steaks and bottles of wine wouldn't suspect her.

Of course the door was unlocked. *Saveme.* Kim was irresponsible and sloppy. *Saveme.* It was practically a sickness with her. *Saveme.* When a friend is sick, you do what you can to help them, she reminded herself. You take care of things for them. *Saveme.* Carrie eased open the car door, hooked a finger under the dog's leather collar, and kissed his head.

"Your head's a little warm, dude. Let's get you into the air-conditioning." She walked Christopher to her car and loaded him into the back seat. *Savemesavemesaveme.* "That's a good boy. That's a nice guy. Let's go." She found a granola bar in her purse, broke it in half, and passed it over the seat. "Hungry?" As she drove away, an excited ease washed over her, sprouting goosebumps on her arms. *Relief.*

# //

# MICHAEL

Elise was thirty years old and she had been sober awhile when she met Michael. Three months, which was the longest she had gone without drugs and alcohol since she was fourteen. Life had gotten much better for Elise in sobriety. "My life is a lot more magical now," she told anyone who asked.

Her home group was in the multi-purpose room of a Catholic church on Wednesday, Friday, and Saturday nights at six p.m. Normally, the kitchen was closed by the time the meeting started, and Elise regularly raided the cabinets and refrigerator when the basket for the "contributions-that-pay-for-the-coffee-and-rental-of-the-room" was passed, acting as if she was stepping out to make a call or go to the bathroom or to get water. There were boxes of Oreos—regular and vanilla—in the pantry and cheese slices and peanut butter and loaves of white bread. She made the church's food her dinner at least twice a week.

Elise had been in a relationship for five months with a woman named Jody who wasn't an addict but had decided to go to meetings and work the steps with Elise anyway. This made Elise see Jody as a codependent person who thought that she was being a supportive person, and Elise wasn't nearly as attracted to

Jody as she had been when she'd been enabling Elise, driving her home from parties and bars and work because she was wasted again and again and again.

On the Friday evening she was due to pick up her 90-day chip, Elise told Jody she needed a night out alone, and that she planned to go to the meeting and then a movie.

"I'll be home by ten or so," she promised. Elise was standing in front of the mirror in their bathroom, putting hot rollers in her long ash-blonde hair.

Jody leaned against the doorframe of the bathroom, watching her girlfriend get ready. "That's good. That's just fine. I'm going to make pasta from scratch again."

Elise shoved a pin around the fat roller at her crown and looked at Jody in the mirror. "It's so gummy. I really prefer the regular boxed kind. Am I gross for that? I'm wrong, huh?"

"Yes." Jody hooked her index finger in the waistband of Elise's jeans and pulled. Elise anchored her hands on the vanity, and Jody kept pulling. "Come here," she laughed, pulling harder.

"I'm late. I want pesto."

Jody let go. "Alright, love. Gummy pesto pasta will be ready when you get home. In the fridge, I suppose."

Elise pulled open the medicine cabinet over the sink and took down a little shot glass that held eyeliner pencils and a tube of mascara. "Mix it up good, okay? Don't just make a puddle of sauce. And no cheese on top. Please." She colored her waterline with a golden-brown pencil and unscrewed the tube of mascara. "Thank you," she remembered to say.

"Yep." Jody took a black eyeliner from the glass and positioned herself next to Elise at the mirror. She held her left eyelid taut and slid the pencil in a neat line near her top lashes. At the corner of her eye, she drew a tiny, precise triangle. She pulled a disposable lighter from her jeans pocket and used it to melt the tip of the pencil, and then ran it over the line, darkening the triangle.

Elise nudged Jody with her elbow. "Get out, show-off."

"I can teach you," Jody offered.

"Out. Love you."

Since she got sober, their relationship had fallen into this rhythm: Elise acting detached and in charge; Jody working hard to earn Elise's attention by waiting on her hand and foot. Jody had framed the prints by Frida Kahlo and Marc Chagall that Elise loved and hung them in the entrance of the one-bedroom apartment she'd lived in for three years, alone, before Elise came home with her one night and then never left. She bought Elise an orchid because she said she wanted one, and then ended up tending to it herself when Elise abandoned it on the windowsill in the living room. Jody cooked healthy meals for the two of them, laying aside her vegetarianism—and the free vegetarian food she used to bring home from the restaurant where she worked—to roast chickens with garlic and red pepper, coating the skin with mayonnaise because her girlfriend liked heavy, fatty food. She folded Elise's clothes and saved her tips and worked extra shifts to see that Elise had the expensive shampoo and body lotion she liked. She did this to keep Elise tethered to their life.

Elise thought Jody was fine as hell, and she worried that one day Jody would get fed up with her tightness and toughness and boundaries and lack of boundaries and kick her out. She could tell that Jody was honest.

Jody was standing at the kitchen counter kneading pasta dough when Elise was ready to leave. Jody's back was turned, and she was concentrating on her work. A soft buzz came from her headphones. Elise looked at Jody for a minute, taking in her long skinny legs and thin shoulders. Jody was wearing what Elise thought of as her uniform, black jeans and a worn black t-shirt. Sometimes the t-shirt was white or gray, and Jody did own a couple of pairs of blue jeans, but everything she owned was the same shape: straight up and down, skinny as a cigarette. She wore black-and-white Adidas Gazelles or Sambas or no shoes at all.

"Honey," Elise said, knowing Jody couldn't hear. "Sweetheart." Jody kept working.

☕

Our Lady Star-of-the-Sea Catholic Church was a mass of 1970's beige bricks, vaguely nautilus-shaped, sliced on every side with narrow stained glass windows depicting cubist representations of Christ and the Virgin Mary. Elise entered through a side door, blessing herself with cold holy water from the glass font on the wall. She stepped into the dark chapel and pulled down the kneeler in the last pew. The cushion squeaked as her knees hit the maroon vinyl cover. She propped her elbows on the back of the pew in front of her, leaning her whole body against the wood and the hymnals stored there. She made her hands into a basket for her face and started to pray. *God: Help me stay sober. Help me make money. Help me be a good girlfriend. Help me lose weight.* She pushed herself up and kicked the kneeler back into place.

Fluorescent light spilled out of the kitchen onto the linoleum floor of the church hall. *Shit,* Elise thought. She checked her pockets for change for the vending machine and decided to suck it up and grab a handful of the cookies next to the coffee pot at the meeting instead. They were always the brittle shortbreads with a hole in the middle she'd eaten at day camp as a kid with apple juice or red Kool-Aid, and their flavor evoked memories of sitting around on concrete in a wet bathing suit, watching for her mother's gray Suburban.

Elise glanced to her right as she passed the kitchen's open double doors and saw a woman in a blue-and-white flannel shirt standing at the counter, leaning over a pile of sandwiches stacked on a cutting board. The woman picked up a wooden-handled cleaver and pressed it into the corner of the top sandwich.

"Easy, now," Elise said from where she was standing at the door. "Any chance I can have one of those?"

"The meeting is in there," the woman laid her index finger

in the middle of the top sandwich and waved the cleaver in the direction of the room across the hall.

"I know that. How do you know I'm going there?"

"Where else would you be going?"

"I might be coming here to help you."

"I've seen you in the meeting. No one is coming to help me with these sandwiches."

"I'm here to help you eat them."

"They're for the fellowship picnic tomorrow. I'm not having one."

"I'll still have one."

"No."

"I've seen you at the meeting, too," Elise said. "Why aren't you there?" Elise could tell that the woman was losing patience. "Your name is Michael. You're an alcoholic."

Michael laughed and then tried to stifle her laughter and hold her face and voice firm. "You're Elise. You're an alcoholic."

"Pleasure," Elise said, lifting her chin in Michael's direction.

"All mine," said Michael.

Elise had two of the ham-and-American-cheese sandwiches on wheat bread Michael was making for the picnic, and then she helped her wrap the rest in plastic and put each one in a brown paper sack with a bag of potato chips and an orange. Eventually she heard the doors across the hall open, and then the sounds of the people talking in the hallway as they left the meeting, and then the hall was completely quiet, and she and Michael were still there talking in the kitchen. In the hour she had meant to be collecting her chip and explaining how she had managed to stay sober for four months, Elise had instead been asking Michael questions and making eyes at her and trying to figure out if she thought that Michael was someone she wanted to be friends with or flirt with or if she could somehow get Michael to mother her or sponsor her in the program—she almost never called the sponsor she'd started with four months earlier.

Elise told Michael about her job as an assistant at a hair salon. Michael told Elise that she had been a Benedictine nun when she was young—just out of high school— and that when she was about Elise's age she'd left the convent because she wanted a family.

"I wanted to be a mother. I couldn't stay."

"Were you secretly in love with a priest?"

"I wasn't in love with anyone."

"So, you just left without a solid plan?"

"No, Elise. My solid plan was to live in the world. I thought I would meet someone I could have a life with, and I wanted to get a job."

"So, your kids are grown?"

"No. I didn't have children."

"Oh, no. Oh man, that's—I'm sorry," Elise brought her index finger to her lips and tapped them as if to push the question back into her mouth. "I'm too nosy. I know that I'm nosy."

Michael passed Elise a rag and began to spray the counters with Formula 409, "Take it away," she said.

Elise walked behind her, swiping the cloth over the surface.

Michael stopped short, looking over her shoulder. "Elbow grease, please. Clean it, don't just play around."

Elise scrubbed harder and then threw the rag into the sink. She turned on the hot tap to rinse it, and as she squeezed it between her hands she said, "Hey, I'm going to the nine thirty movie if you want to come with," she turned to face Michael, who was combining extra slices of three loaves of wheat bread into one plastic bag. "We can sneak some Oreos," she walked over to the cookie cabinet and opened the doors, "do you know where the ziplocks are?"

"You should go on home," Michael said to Elise, still looking down at the bread bag. "I'm going too."

"I don't want to. I need some alone time."

"You invited me to the movies just now." Michael twisted the bag and tied a knot in the end.

"I need personal time." She took down a box of sandwich-size ziplocks and waved them at Michael. "Found them," she took down a brand-new package of Oreos and peeled it open. "Hello, beautiful," she said into the tray of cookies, and took a couple of inches of them between her thumb and index finger and dropped them in the bag.

"I need to go home, but maybe we can do that another time."

Elise turned to Michael and frowned in a joking way. "Alright, I guess."

"I'll see you at the meeting," Michael said, pulling a ring of keys from a peg on the wall. "Do you need a ride?"

"No, I still have my license. I never got a DUI."

"Good for you. My number is on the meeting phone list," Michael clicked off the switches that controlled the fluorescent lights in the back of the vast kitchen. "Call if you need anything," she clicked off the lights in the front of the kitchen, where she and Elise were standing. "If you think you want to take a drink." The only light in the room was a shaft of red from the exit sign in the hallway, just past where Michael stood holding the door open with one foot.

"This is my cue to leave, I guess," Elise laughed, shoving the ziplock into her pocket and slipping past Michael, who locked the kitchen door behind them.

"I'm just not that hungry." Elise lifted the foil covering a plate of brownies Jody had made as a surprise to celebrate Elise's four months of sobriety. It was midnight, and Jody had waited up.

"That's different for you," Jody said, stretching her arms over her head so that the white tanktop she was wearing inched up, exposing her navel and ribs.

Elise pinched Jody's side, "Don't be a dick."

"I just meant that brownies are your favorite."

"You know I'm funny about that stuff." Elise raised an eyebrow, and then flipped the corner of the foil covering the plate again with her index fingernail. She broke off the edge of a brownie and put it in her mouth. "This is so good. I'm not even hungry."

"You don't have to do that," Jody said.

"I know. Hey, look," she pressed the foil into the side of the plate, "I met this woman tonight at the meeting."

"Okay."

"She used to be a nun, and she's in the program."

"Alright. So, Michael."

"Yes! Yeah, yeah, yeah," Elise grabbed at Jody's hands. "I like that lady."

"She's been sober a long time. Are you going to ask her to sponsor you? You haven't called Helen lately."

"No, I want to be friends with her. I just want to hang out."

"With Michael?"

"Yeah," Elise said. She took another brownie and went into the bathroom and took off her makeup with the expensive cleanser from Sephora that Jody had surprised her with for no reason.

Elise didn't miss a meeting for three straight weeks after that first evening with Michael, and she even started calling Helen every day again because Michael reminded her to do that.

"Just a suggestion," Michael said, shrugging one shoulder and sort of smiling into her lap. She looked up at Elise and laid a hand lightly on Elise's arm. "It works for me. I still call my sponsor every day."

"Poor Helen. I abandoned her a while ago. After my first ninety days." Elise could feel a muscle under her right eye jumping. "I'm going to get some coffee. Do you want some?"

"Yes."

She poured powdered cream into the bottom of two short styrofoam cups and tore open a Sweet n' Low. She divided the contents of the pink packet between the two cups, a little in this one, a little in that one. She knew that Michael liked her coffee just a tiny bit sweet and she had started drinking her own that way. No sense in throwing away half a packet of perfectly good poison. She'd seen Michael fold the top of a Sweet n' Low closed and shove it in her pocket once. The coffee pot was full, and a raft of tiny bubbles floated on the surface. She grabbed a couple of napkins and carried the cups back to her seat next to Michael.

Elise had learned a lot about Michael since they started sitting together at meetings. She knew that Michael was a vegetarian and a Libra and a smoker (Camel Lights). Michael smelled like Gain laundry detergent and she wore the same few items of clothing all the time. The jeans and flannel she'd been wearing that night in the kitchen, plus a pair of cream-colored twill trousers, a black turtleneck, and a handful of long-sleeved pocket t-shirts in various shades of gray seemed to comprise the rest of her wardrobe. Every single time Elise saw her Michael was wearing Birkenstocks—dark-brown, nubuck Arizonas. Elise dug her old, light-brown, suede Arizonas out of the back of her closet and started wearing them again with argyle socks. It was winter, and Michael wore socks with her sandals too.

"Can I be nosy?" Elise asked Michael one evening as they walked to their cars after a meeting. It was nearly eight pm, but barely dark and starting to feel like summer.

"I thought you weren't going to do that anymore," Michael said and looped her arm through Elise's. They had gotten comfortable with touching each other with a sort of heightened platonic warmth, a familiarity that Elise gauged was somewhere on the level of the camaraderie she shared with her older sisters but tinged with a faint charge she recognized as desire.

"I wasn't, but I keep thinking about your other life in the convent. I keep wondering what kind of nun you were."

"I was a Benedictine. I thought I told you that."

"No, no, like who you were back then. What you were thinking."

Michael fished her car keys out of her pocket and pressed the button on the fob that unlocked her white Honda Civic. "Look, I'm going to get a cigarette."

"I want one," Elise called after her. "Hey—"

"Hang on." Michael rummaged through her car's console and fished out a fresh pack of cigarettes. She tapped the pack against her palm.

"I want one," Elise said again.

"You don't."

"So, what were you thinking? What was your plan?"

"Elise, I don't remember—"

Elise interrupted her, "Hey, how old are you?"

"How old do you think I am?" Michael walked over to Elise and handed her the cigarette she was smoking. Elise dragged on it and tilted her chin up to blow a plume of smoke into the air.

"I like older women," Elise said.

"I'm old enough to be your mother."

"You're not anybody's mother, sweetheart." Elise squeezed Michael's waist.

Michael threw the cigarette onto the asphalt and crushed it with her toe. She faced Elise, taking her by the elbows. Looking into Elise's eyes, she said, "When you say things like that and call me sweetheart, it makes me think you want something that I just don't have to give you, Elise." She let her hands fall to her sides. "You're just starting to become a really good sober person. It would be wrong for me to interfere with any part of that."

Elise felt a big, cheesy smile come over her face as she cast her eyes on the flattened cigarette on the ground. She was mortified. "I just like you, I'm sorry. I'm not sorry. I'm attracted to you. I can't help it."

"That's fine, but I can't be in your life that way. You have that in your life already, and I'm afraid you're trying to fuck it up so you can feel something exciting."

"Jody and I are winding down, okay? 'It's' not going to last much longer."

"Go home, Elise." Michael started walking toward her car. "Go home and see your girlfriend."

Elise spent the entire drive home devising ways to break up with Jody that wouldn't mess up either of their lives too much.

She could say she needed to live alone for her sobriety. She could relapse for a minute and get sober again once she'd found another place to live. She could blame their relationship for the slip and this would make Jody feel bad. Jody would want her to do what she needed to do to stay sober. Jody would help her find a different apartment and she would even help Elise move and get settled because Jody was a good person, and Elise knew that Jody loved her. She might even see the logic, eventually, of Elise falling in love with Michael, and how that could somehow keep her sober.

When Elise got home Jody was there, fiddling with a recipe for garlic shrimp.

"I can't put curry in this, right?" Jody kissed the top of Elise's head. "You smell like cigarettes." She held Elise's long ponytail to her nose. "I like that smell. Were you smoking?"

"No. Someone was smoking near me. Someone blew smoke in my direction."

"Someone?" Jody wrapped her arms around Elise's waist and held her in place.

"No one you know."

Elise leaned into Jody and Jody bit Elise's earlobe, and then her neck.

Of course they fucked.

They tore at each other like a couple of wolves until midnight. At one point, Elise heard her phone buzz on the bedside table. She ignored it and closed her eyes, getting into the feeling of Jody's fingers inside her. It buzzed again minutes later, and then again.

"Hang on," she said, and checked it.

I need to talk to you

the first message said.

The next:

I can't stop thinking about you

Then:

> I want to put my arms around you.

Elise laid the phone aside and looked down between her legs, where Jody was running her tongue along the crease between her hipbone and inner thigh, "Michael says hi."

Jody plunged into Elise, staring her down as Elise gasped and met Jody's mouth with a tilt of her pelvis.

Later, Elise got up to pee and decided to take a bath. She texted Michael.

> We can meet. That's ok.

> When and where.

Elise swirled the washrag in the hot water and took down a bottle of lavender Dr. Bronner's. She poured some onto the rag and started soaping her body. She ducked under the water, scraping her hair back. Coming up for air, she rubbed her eyes hard, luxuriating in the feeling. She texted Michael.

> You say when and where.

> The kitchen? 9 tomorrow morning.

> Yep.

# III

# EVERYBODY GETS A LITTLE CRUSH SOMETIMES

Elise stopped at the chapel before she met Michael. There was a Mass at seven-thirty each morning, and the scent of incense still hung in the air. A woman in a mint green cardigan knelt in the second pew near the front, thumbing the black beads of her rosary. Elise sat across from her, directly in front of the gold monstrance with the exposed Eucharist. She fixed her eyes on the host and let herself zone out. Growing up, she had been taught to take her problems to Holy Communion.

"Put it in the cup"—was what her mother would say to Elise and her sister Carrie when they were heartbroken or anxious or wanted something badly that they thought they might not get— and she meant it literally. When they took a sip of Communion wine they were to think of their problem, whatever it was, and surrender it to Christ the moment the blessed wine touched their lips. "And then you forget about it," her mother told them. "Let Him have it."

Elise wondered if she should put her relationship with Michael in the cup. She had put lots of hurts and worries into the cup over the years, and they had all solved themselves; the details of every single one of them escaped her now. She stared at the host a little longer, letting her eyes relax and settle on the cross etched faintly into the middle of the wafer.

Michael wasn't in the kitchen when Elise arrived, so she snapped on the lights and made a pot of coffee. She was stirring half-and-half into a cup when Michael texted to say she was running late. She didn't answer. Elise was untwisting a peanut butter cracker from a box she'd found in the pantry when Michael walked in, looking flushed.

"Your face is all red." Michael walked over to Elise and took the two halves of the peanut butter cracker from her hands.

"Hey." Elise's eyes followed Michael's hand tossing the crackers into the trash.

Michael turned back to Elise, taking her now empty hands in her own.

Elise looked down. "You like to hold both hands at once, don't you?"

Michael stepped closer and brought Elise's hands behind her own back, so that Elise's arms were circling her waist. "This feels good."

Elise pulled Michael close. When they kissed, she tasted cigarettes. She followed Michael in her car to the apartment where Michael lived, about a mile from the church. Michael had the top floor of a three-story pink-and-white Queen Anne, a studio that ran the length of the house at the top of a broad mahogany staircase.

*Michael still lives like a nun,* Elise thought upon first seeing the space. No couch. A round pine table with a single cane-back chair held a clunky HP laptop; a green glass ashtray; and a coffee mug with the words "Pensacola Beach" written in juicy yellow script over a cresting cartoon wave—these occupied an alcove near the galley kitchen, where three long boards mounted on the wall next to the sink stood in for a pantry. The top shelf was lined with glass jars of what looked like coarse salt and rolled oats and olive oil. Crowded together on the far side of the bottom shelf was a set of three plain white dinner plates, topped with a stack of plain white saucers and a nest of three neat white bowls. A pint glass on the counter held a clutch of jumbled forks and spoons.

"That's a twin bed." Elise pointed at the narrow mattress on a metal frame in the far corner of the room, positioned to the side of a bay window facing the street. She walked over to the bed and put her keys and jacket on the pink cotton spread and pressed her hands into the mattress, as if she were testing the springs. The white-painted frame creaked and shifted. She looked up at Michael, still standing in the doorway. "Uh-oh," she said, smiling through the curtain of her hair.

Of course they fucked.

The intensity of Michael's kisses surprised Elise, and the way that Michael held the back of her head—while she edged her toward the bed kissing her—was something Elise didn't really like, but the kisses turned into soft biting she did not mind at all, and the way that Michael whipped off her flannel and jeans in five flat seconds delighted her. When Michael gave Elise's dress the same treatment—grasping the hem and pulling it over Elise's head in one swift motion—she was so turned on that she threw back the covers and fell in pulling Michael on top of her.

Elise drove home in bright afternoon sunlight, convinced that leaving Jody was the right thing to do. She knew that seeing Jody would make her weak, so she packed a couple of outfits and a swimsuit and her makeup and went to her mother's house for the weekend. She left Jody a note.

### At my Mom's. Call you in the AM.

She balled up the paper and threw it away. This would never do. Jody would be on her like gravy on rice. She'd know something was wrong and call until Elise answered. She tried again.

### I'm at my Mom's. Let's talk tomorrow.

She ripped the paper into strips and threw them in the trash with the other note. One more time.

## At my Mom's. PMSing hard. Leave me be.

She left.

Over the next couple of days, Jody sent Elise sweet, supportive text messages with pictures of Schnauzers and a link to a
podcast about sobriety. She sent a meme with a Brené Brown
quote and a picture of a black-and-white striped bikini; she was
at Target, asking if Elise wanted a new swimsuit.
    Elise answered.

> Ummm ok . . .

> Size 8 top and 12 bottom.
> Just break up two sets
> Jody.

> I do it all the time.

Then Elise texted Michael and drove by her house a few times.
    Michael wanted to see Elise again, but not until she'd ended
things with Jody.

> We can't do that again
> until you're free.

> I saw her at the meeting
> and had to pretend I was
> having an allergy attack.

> Tell her.

Elise was surprised and totally delighted by Michael's ardor.
She thought Michael would put her off or change her mind,
but it seemed like the opposite was happening. It seemed like
Michael wanted her.

> I'll talk to her this
> weekend.

> I'll talk to her soon.

> Which? This weekend or soon?

> This weekend.

Elise was on fire. She called Jody.

Elise knew anger was Jody's main intoxicant, ever since Jody'd stopped drinking to support Elise. In those four months, Jody unloaded on their neighbor for playing video games with the volume up late at night and broke a hairdryer by slamming it on the bathroom counter when it shorted out while she was using it. She cursed at her computer when it was slow, at the food in the refrigerator when it went bad, and the windshield wipers on her truck when they didn't move fast enough in a sudden rainstorm. Each time one of these outbursts occurred, she'd cried and apologized to Elise, berating herself for losing control. Elise always shrugged it off; she was comfortable with anger. "I get pissed off all the time," she'd say. She knew Jody wouldn't ever hurt her physically. But her confession about her afternoon with Michael made Jody angry in a way Elise had never seen. Jody got quiet.

They met up at a coffee shop they both liked. It had a spacious pine deck that Elise assumed would give them some privacy. She didn't want to talk to Jody at their apartment or at her mother's house.

They sat across from one another at a wrought iron café table. Elise took a long swallow of her iced tea and launched in. "I need to get some space from this. I'm fucking up. I did something. With someone."

Jody leaned back in her chair and looked away. "Uh-oh. Something with someone. That sounds serious. You have a little crush now? Is it Denise?"

Denise was the video-game neighbor and Elise had made

no secret of the fact that she thought Denise was good looking and arrogant about it, which attracted her more.

"No. Not Denise."

"Who have you been flirting with, then? Who have you been kissing? You can say, Elise. You don't have to run off." Jody grabbed Elise's fingers across the table and kissed them. "Everybody gets a little crush sometimes."

"It's not like that. It's Michael."

"Who's he?"

"Michael. From the place. With the people. The meeting. Michael."

"Michael from the program. Like, Michael who's sixty years old?"

"She's past that, I think. Yeah, Michael."

Jody wanted to know all of the *hows* and the *whys* of it all, and Elise told her some of it.

"You slept together," Jody said, slowly. "And now you want to be with her."

"Yes," Elise said, looking into her lap. She picked at the threads on her cutoffs.

"And you want our relationship to end. So you can do that."

"Yes."

They agreed that Elise would come and move her stuff the next day, when Jody was at work, and pay the landlord to have the locks replaced. Jody looked away from Elise. "I can't look at you right now." She dug her keys out of her pocket and pulled the lid off her plastic cup of iced coffee. She knocked back what was left in the cup and placed it on the table, upside down. She smashed it flat with her open palm, and then walked to her car and drove away.

Elise texted Michael.

> Okay I told her. Can I see you now?

Michael texted back.

> Come now

and Elise drove to Michael's apartment and stayed there until the next morning.

☕

Elise's mother called her phone at 7 am and kept calling until Elise picked up. "There's an awful lot of your things on my front walk, Elise."

She sat up in bed. "What things?"

"I see some dresses and a bag of makeup. Books. Your jewelry box. Wide open."

"Oh." *Jody.*

"Do you know anything about this?"

"Yeah."

"Come and see about it, please. Right now, before the neighborhood gets an eyeful."

"Can't you bring it inside? Just leave it in the front hall, okay?"

"Absolutely not. See you soon." Her mother hung up.

Elise flopped back in bed. "Jody left my stuff in my mom's front yard."

Michael's eyes widened, "Oh, no."

"It's okay," she pulled Michael into her chest and kissed the top of her head. "I deserve this. I can handle this." She ran her fingers down Michael's back and squeezed her hip. Michael turned over and went back to sleep.

Elise got dressed and collected her car keys and cigarettes and her lighter. She took a can of Diet Coke from the refrigerator and left a note for Michael on the kitchen counter. *Lunch? Call me.* She signed with a capital E and a sketch of a pizza slice. She eased the door to Michael's apartment closed so that she wouldn't disturb her sleep. At the end of the hall, the door to the street was jammed and she had to shove it open. When she did, a stack of paperback books that had been blocking it slid down the stairs. She collected them under her arm as she descended, trying not to spill her soda: *The Tibetan Book of Living and*

*Dying; Many Lives, Many Masters; I, Tina.* A faded yellow sweatshirt with an image of a cow skull and the words "Santa Fe" printed on the front was wadded up on the sidewalk, along with a box of jasmine tea and two strands of plastic turquoise and coral-colored beads.

She texted Jody.

> Look, I know you're upset, but this stuff you left at Michael's isn't mine—it's yours. Just give me a minute and I'll come and get the rest of my things and return this stuff to you. I have to go clean up the other mess you made at my mom's first. THANKS A LOT WHAT THE FUCK.

She stacked the books on the sidewalk and placed the box of tea and the necklaces on top. She pulled the sweatshirt on and got everything in her car.

Jody texted her back.

> Those aren't my things.

> They're Michael's.

# IV

## MIND ME

Carrie loved the home she and her wife Kim shared. There were three bedrooms in a split floor plan, and a granite counter-top kitchen in the middle. A nice Sub-Zero refrigerator in the kitchen. The laundry room was next to her bedroom and the bathroom had two sinks. Since they were getting divorced, the living room and front hall were piled with empty boxes for Carrie to pack with whatever she felt like taking. Kim had told her to take anything she wanted. It was Kim's house: she had made the down payment and she paid the monthly note. The thought of packing to move drained Carrie, so to prepare herself, she decided to spend a thousand dollars of her wife's money on new clothes.

She started with lingerie. She let the saleslady at Dillard's fill a dressing room with the Wacoal and Le Mystere bras she liked and normally only allowed herself to buy one at a time, every couple of years. "These are good," she said, passing three of each over the dressing room door. "I like all of these. Hang on to them, please."

The woman's beige plastic name tag read "Vanessa" in black capital letters. Vanessa wore her dark hair in a shag and was probably thirty or thirty-one, a decade younger than Carrie.

Vanessa's two front teeth crossed slightly, Carrie noticed, and she wore a silky-looking wrap dress printed with red-and-violet paisley. She wrapped Carrie's purchases in tissue paper and slid them into a slick plastic bag, careful not to let anything shift or crumple.

"Thank you, Vanessa. Thank you for helping me. Your dress is very cool."

Vanessa gave a closed-mouth smile, which to Carrie was unfortunate; she thought that wonky teeth were hot.

Carrie took the bag and rode the escalator to the first floor of the store. She walked over to the Chanel counter and sprayed the tester of Miss Dior on her neck and wrists. She sprayed a little in her hair.

When she got home from the underwear binge, she threw all her new stuff in a mesh bag and set it washing on cold with Woolite. She fixed herself a peanut-butter-and-jelly sandwich and took it to the guest bedroom and closed the door. She removed her silver hoop earrings and tossed them onto the dresser and picked through the books she and Kim had arranged on the petite antique mahogany bookshelf Carrie had bought on a trip to see Kim's mother in New Orleans.

Carrie was proud of the collection that they'd curated and displayed for the visitors that occasionally came to stay (Kim's nieces, Carrie's friends): slim volumes of contemporary poetry; everything by Garcia Marquez; everything by Zadie Smith. In the next moment she was embarrassed by her pride because she couldn't stand it when people were pleased with themselves. Early in their relationship she'd seen a post of Kim's on Instagram, a picture of Kim's feet and lower legs, crossed at the ankles, showing off a brand-new pair of John Fluevog oxfords. Carrie seriously considered ghosting on Kim at that moment, but decided that this could be one of the trade-offs she'd heard her friends in healthy relationships describing. They put up with much more troublesome trade-offs—like questionable dental hygiene and terrible taste in music.

Carrie pulled down a book of poems she loved, *Slow*

*Lightning* by Eduardo C. Corral. She read "Watermark" a couple of times, slowly, and then began emptying the shelves into the half-dozen wine cartons she'd scavenged from the loading dock of a liquor store downtown. Those were the best for packing heavy books, she knew.

Carrie and Kim had been together for three years when they got married. The ceremony was at the public library on a Monday at nine am, when they knew it would be empty. Carrie wore an ivory sheath, camel heels, and Chanel No. 5, and Kim wore skinny black pants and a black button up. Ck One (another trade-off). They both wore Rosewood lipstick by Laura Mercier. Carrie hadn't asked permission from the library when she'd planned the wedding, just invited Kim's cousin Liz, who officiated, plus two friends to witness the ceremony, which was held in the fiction stacks, in front of Sarah Waters's novels. Carrie made sure to stand so that *Tipping the Velvet* would be in the pictures Liz took after the ceremony. Kim wanted whatever Carrie wanted, which is why they didn't get married in front of new non-fiction. She had bought the same wedding set for Carrie and herself, one plain platinum band, thin and delicate as silk thread, and one wider, sturdier one, with three inset diamonds. Carrie liked the starkness of the sets, and the fact that they were flat and identical. They took everyone out for coffee and donuts afterward and Liz, who Carrie loved because she was wild, flirted relentlessly with Kim's invited guest, a man who had coached Kim through a couple of marathons in the years before she and Carrie met. This went on until Kim passed out a round of espresso shots in to-go cups, and then she and Carrie went home and took off their wedding clothes and took a long nap.

Carrie stacked the boxes of books in the trunk of her car and drove to her mother's house. Her sister Elise was in the backyard floating on her back on a raft in the swimming pool wearing one of their mother's bathing suits, a black strapless one-piece that was at least two sizes too large.

"Oh, that's a pretty swimsuit, sister," Carrie called to Elise, who lifted a can of Diet Coke in Carrie's direction.

"Ain't it something?" Elise hitched up the front of the suit, which had bagged down into her cleavage. Elise was ten years younger than Carrie, a "surprise" her parents had welcomed in their early forties.

"Sure is."

They laughed a little, and Elise paddled one-handed over to the side of the pool, where Carrie was standing. "Mom's at church. Can I borrow those sunglasses?" She waved the can at Carrie's face.

"Don't ruin them." Carrie took off the tortoise Wayfarers Kim had given her for her birthday the year before and handed them to her sister. "You know what, never mind. Keep them."

Elise smiled and put the glasses on, "Thanks, babe." She pushed off the side of the pool with her foot. "These are prescription, Miss," she shouted after Carrie, who had turned to walk into the house.

"You know what they say about beggars and choosers, Miss," Carrie answered. "Just don't wear them to drive."

Elise made them laugh and she confounded them all with her money problems and her romance problems and her drug and alcohol problems. Their mother regularly fished pregnancy tests out of the garbage can in the bathroom attached to Elise's old bedroom, where she still landed occasionally, for weeks or months at a time. The tests were always negative, but Carrie knew that their mother was terrified that a day would come when the result would be different. She'd called Carrie crying one Saturday morning after another one of these discoveries.

"I can't raise another baby, Carrie, I'm too old. I'm seventy years old. Talk to your sister, please."

"Stay out of her trash then—and mind your own business. Buy a box of condoms and put it on her bed if you're really that worried."

"I would never."

"Then give her the money for it. If she were your son, you'd put a little cash on her dresser and tell her to be careful. And stop thinking about raising any child of Elise's. She won't be having a baby any time soon. Besides, seventy is not that old."

When Elise started dating women, their mother called Carrie, furious, and accused her of setting a bad example for Elise. Carrie hung up on her mid-sentence and didn't speak to their mother or Elise for a year.

Now their mother's kitchen smelled like her chicken spaghetti sauce. Carrie lifted the lid of the crockpot on the counter, which was full of what she knew was jarred sauce doctored up with chopped bell peppers and onions. She took a teaspoon from the drawer and started dredging up little pieces of the chicken her mother always added, whole, to the pot. "Ooh, I want this," she said out loud to the empty kitchen. Chicken spaghetti was her favorite. She scooped some of the meat and sauce into a bowl and ate it like soup, standing over the kitchen sink. She took another bowlful and ate that, too. She ran water in the bowl and then drove herself to Our Lady-Star-of-the-Sea and parked next to her mother's car. She took out her phone and opened the notes app.

- I want to be loved ardently
- I want to love ardently
- I want to be loved gently
- I want to love gently
- I want to be loved tenderly
- I want to tenderly love

She texted her mother.

> I need to sleep at your house for awhile

That's fine.

> I'm out here in the parking lot can you meet me

Ok. 5 mins.

Really 5?

Carrie enough.

She rolled down the window and opened the banking app on her phone. For the past three weeks, since she'd discovered Kim's many infidelities, Carrie'd been transferring money to her savings from the household account she and Kim shared, and it had almost a thousand dollars now.

Her mother appeared at the car window. "Oh, it's you."

"Oh, it's you," Carrie answered. "It's you again. They let you in there like that?" Carrie gestured at her mother's sleeveless shift. "I can see your arms, Annie. Both of them." She raised an eyebrow.

"I have a scarf in my bag," her mother fanned herself with a bulletin. "Now what? What's wrong now, Carrie?"

"Nothing. I just need a change of scenery."

"Well, go on and pack a bag. Elise is there."

"I know that."

"I can't have you both there for long, alright?" Her mother worked the fan a little harder.

"I know."

Carrie's mother had made her old bedroom into a sewing room, a place where she stored her plastic Singer machine from the '60's and tackle box of sewing supplies, along with many other things she seldom used. There was a treadmill against one wall, facing Carrie's old tv/vhs combo machine. Stacked around it were tapes of the movies Carrie had been obsessed with in high school: *Heathers, The Breakfast Club, Pretty in Pink*, along with a couple of workout videos. Her twin-sized trundle bed was still situated under the east-facing window, covered in the tea-rose-print Laura Ashley comforter she'd picked out for her fifteenth birthday. She threw her bag on top of the bed. A jack-and-jill bathroom separated her room from Elise's, and she could hear the shower running behind the closed door on her side. She knocked.

"Hi. May I?"

"Just a minute." The water stopped and Elise slid the door open. She was wrapped in a pink towel, her hair tied in a sloppy bundle on top of her head. "I heard you were coming to stay."

"Just for a little while." Carrie looked past Elise into the bathroom. "I need to get in here."

"Alright, alright," Elise said, backing into her bedroom.

"Look, can I sleep in your room tonight?" she unzipped her jeans and sat down to pee.

"If you want."

Elise's room hadn't changed much since she'd graduated high school a dozen years earlier, mostly because she'd continued to occupy it intermittently for that entire time. Two twin beds were set in an L shape against the walls opposite the bathroom door. One was neatly made with a silky black bedspread. The other was a wreck, sheets twisted and sliding onto the floor where a pile of dirty clothes, including the still-wet bathing suit she'd been wearing earlier, lay next to an abandoned game of solitaire. A bookshelf crammed with framed photos of Elise and her friends, half-burned candles, and an assortment of outsized photography and art books stood opposite the beds. Elise was sitting on the floor in front of a full-length mirror applying back eyeliner in a thin, upturned swoop.

"Cat-eye. How original. Let me guess, red lipstick?" Carrie nudged her sister's makeup bag, resting on the floor, with her toe.

"Jealous," Elise said, smiling broadly into the mirror as she tapped cream blush onto the apples of her cheeks.

"I am jealous," Carrie said, kicking off her buff-colored suede flats and flopping, belly down, onto one of the beds. "I wish I was young. I wish I could still just go out and make somebody want me."

"Excuse me," Elise caught Carrie's eye in the mirror. "Your wife wants you, obviously. Look at how she's got you living. I would love that, man. Why are you here, anyway?"

"I'm mad at Kim," she said. "We're over."

"What did you do?" Elise asked eagerly, turning around to face her sister.

"Nothing. She's been stepping out."

"No way."

"She has. I talked to one of them."

"*One* of them?"

"She's been at it awhile."

Carrie told Elise what she knew of Kim's affairs, and that she planned to divorce Kim. She'd hired a lawyer, and Kim had, too.

"Does Annie know?' Elise whispered.

"Absolutely not. Carrie pushed herself onto an elbow. "You know how she is. That would really complicate things here," she hiked a thumb over her shoulder, indicating their mother, who she presumed was outside Elise's bedroom with her ear to a juice a glass pressed to the door, "and I am quite sure I'm not up for it."

"You should pray for Kim," Elise said, pulling a silky black tank top over her head.

"Elise, you need to wear a bra with top. And stop trying to do religion on me. You know I don't like that."

"You need to turn your anger over before it eats you alive."

"I said to stop. You sound like AA."

"I hate bras." Elise plucked a pair of cut-offs from the dirty clothes on the floor. The bathing suit had left a wet spot on the right leg near the pocket; she pressed at it with her hands.

"Run the blow dryer on it," Carrie said. "You know what? On second thought, enjoy your sky-high boobies now, while you can. Things do change."

"Can I wear those?" Elise pointed at Carrie's flats.

"No."

Carrie straightened up her sister's bedroom and settled in. She found two sets of clean, white, twin sheets in the hall closet, and she stripped the beds and washed the comforters and the pile of dirty clothes on the floor, which smelled like cigarette smoke and Big Red gum. She stacked the playing cards together and put Elise's makeup bag in a drawer in the bathroom. The drawer also contained: a pack of Big Red gum, a holy card with a picture of Saint Sebastian that made Carrie wince (he was tied to a tree and shot full of arrows), a bunch of loose ponytail holders, and a bottle of Advil. She went through the rest of the drawers until she found a bottle of painkillers prescribed by their family dentist. She took out two pills and washed them down with water from the tap.

Her mother knocked on the door and began to open it as Carrie was getting into her pajamas, a white t-shirt that brushed the top of her thighs. "Oop, sorry," her mother backed out, looking away.

"Mom, you can come in. I'm decent."

"I'll wait until you have your nightie on."

Carrie rolled her eyes. "Okay, so, I don't do that anymore. Come on in." She peeled back the covers on one of the twin beds and sat with her back against the wall, wadding the sheets around her crossed legs.

Her mother opened the door wider but kept her eyes on the floor. "Do you need anything?"

"How about some tea? And maybe a piece of toast. With cheese."

Her mother looked up and smiled. "Ok. I was thinking more along the lines of clean towels, but I can do that."

"Thanks, Annie."

"Mom to you. Mom will do. I want to talk to you about something first." She tightened the belt of her robe. "Can we talk for a minute?"

"No way, baby. I need that snack and then I need to get some beauty sleep. Tomorrow? Tomorrow, okay?"

Her mother brought Carrie a mug of tea with a lemon wedge floating on its steaming surface. She set that on the nightstand, along with a saucer that held one piece of toasted white bread that she'd spread with margarine and then covered with a slice of American cheese torn into strips. "Here you go, mademoiselle."

Carrie reached for the mug and took a long sip. "Merci beaucoup." She knew that the painkillers would kick in soon, making her drowsy and relaxed. She wanted to be alone with a book and her tea when that happened.

"You can stay here for as long as you want. I like having you and your sister here."

"Thank you. I know that."

"I want you to stay." Her mother tapped Carrie's knee.

"I know, Mom."

"You have to mind me, though."

"I'll pick up after myself, don't worry about that." She pulled the covers tighter around herself.

"That's not what I mean." Annie sat down on the side of the bed and faced Carrie. "I want you to start living right."

Carrie set her tea on the bedside table and lifted her chin in the direction of the bedroom door. "Go. I am trying to relax right now and I don't need this."

"I want to see you back in church, and I want you to meet someone and settle down. Someone who is right for you."

"Mama, that's not ever going to be a man. We've talked about this."

Annie got up and walked toward the door. "That can change. Ask your sister. She's been in church every week —"

"AA is not the same as church. Her meeting happens to be there—"

"No, she's been going to Mass and seeing a man she met there."

"You are mistaken. Elise is gay, too, and you know that.

She's probably here because she hit a rough patch with her girlfriend."

"That's not right. She's seeing someone she met at church now. His name is Michael."

Carrie could see the strain in her mother's face, and the hope. She felt the pills begin to fuzz her mind a bit, and she wanted to let go and let that feeling take over her whole body. She wanted to read the *Vanity Fair* she'd shoved in her purse as she'd walked out the door that afternoon, and drink her tea. "Okay, Mom. Okay," she put her hands up in surrender. "I will talk to Elise." She pulled the saucer holding the piece of toast onto her lap and reached for the cup of tea, now cool enough to drink. She took a sip. "Goodnight, Annie."

"Mom, please. Mom is just fine. Goodnight, baby. God bless you."

"Okay."

# V

## MON DIEU, LOVE

"Almonds, Oreos, peanut butter and jelly. Grape jelly. Orange juice, tampons, razors, but not Bic razors, the nice ones with lotion. Ranch dressing, strawberry yogurt, candy. You need to tell me what kind of candy. Gum. You said peppermint Orbit. Cough drops. Those are for me. Carmex for me. Okay, Elise. What else?" Michael was sitting at the kitchen table making a list of things to keep in her studio apartment. To make Elise happy. "Did you say tampons?"

Elise was lying in bed across the room reading Michael's copy of *Many Lives, Many Masters*. "Yes. Super, okay? Not regular and not super-plus. Super in the yellow box."

"Super in the yellow box," Michael made a note on the list in front of her. "Okay, which candy?"

"Just, you know."

"M&M's? Peanut M&M's."

"No, something nice, from Whole Foods. The good peanut butter cups and cinnamon Taza. And salted almond. And the spicy one."

"Right."

"Hey, do you believe in this?" She waved the book in Michael's direction.

"Yes. Get dressed and come with me," Michael walked over to the bed and sat down. "I want to be with you all day."

Elise pressed the book into her stomach, over the covers, "My period. I'm sleepy."

Michael pushed the book aside and put her hands on Elise's hipbones. "Listen. Just get out of bed and put on the dress you wore yesterday. That's easy, easy, easy. I'll make coffee."

"No." Elise pulled Michael on top of her.

"I'll take you out for coffee then," she said into Elise's neck.

"No."

"Whatever," Michael said. Before she left the apartment, Michael texted Jody.

> I'm running errands. Come with?

She pulled out of the driveway. She checked her phone at the stop sign at the end of the street:

At the stoplight in front of the courthouse:

In the grocery store parking lot, bubbles:

Bubbles.

Bubbles.

Bubbles.

Bubbles bubbles bubbles.

. . . Okay. Pick me up?

Be right over.

As soon as Michael left, Elise leaned over and felt around under the bed for a shoebox she'd found there the day before while she was looking for an earring she'd dropped when she was getting undressed. She hooked her finger into its side and dragged it into the light. The box was overflowing with folded paper and dozens of photographs. Pictures of Michael.

Pictures of Michael on her 50th birthday. Her 55th. Her 60th. Pictures of Michael with her girlfriend Louise, who she lived with for fifteen years, some of the '80s and all of the '90s. Some of her thirties and all of her forties. A black-and-white picture of Michael and her three younger brothers on the deck of their father's shrimp boat, all in cutoff shorts and white rubber boots. Michael's t-shirt was printed with a fierce-looking panther and the words St. Francis Cabrini Elementary School on the front. A picture of a teenage Michael in a long baby-blue satin gown and tiara, with a red-and-white satin sash with the words Miss Lafourche Parish 1970 spelled out in silver glitter. Pictures of Michael in the aughts at Mardi Gras, on New Year's Eve, at the French Quarter Festival, at a Saints' game, sitting on the steps of the house she rented in the Bywater for two years after she left Louise for one of their close friends.

Elise knew that before she was Michael, her name had been Bernadette. Elise separated the pictures into two piles: Bernadette and Michael. Before the convent and after.

"You already had a primo Catholic name," she'd pressed one evening after dinner, "why didn't you just keep Bernadette?"

"It doesn't work like that. You have to choose a new name and I liked the name Michael. I still like it."

"You seem to. Did you ever want to take back Bernadette? Like, after you left?"

"No. By then I'd been Michael for a while. I wanted to keep being Michael."

"I'm trying to think of a name I'd want if it was me."

"Why are you thinking of that?" Michael stood up and collected their empty dishes and walked to the kitchen sink. "I'm surprised you and your sister don't have saints' names. Your upbringing."

"Who said we don't? We have saints' names. Carrie's first name is Mary."

"Mary Carrie?" Michael stood at the sink with her back to Elise. "What?"

"Her middle name is Catherine and she prefers Carrie. You're rude," Elise laughed. "My mother's first name is Mary, too."

"Why Annie, then?" Michael asked.

"Her middle name is Annette."

Michael turned toward Elise, her hands covered in soapsuds, "Your mother's name is Mary Annette? Are you serious? Do you hear that?" She shook her head and returned to the dishes. "What's your middle name?"

"What do you think it is? I don't even want to tell you now. You're being awful."

"I guess I think it's Mary."

"It's Lucy."

"Oh, a grisly one."

"I know. Those poor blue eyes on a dish." Elise walked over to Michael and wrapped her arms around her waist. She hooked her chin over Michael's shoulder. "What's your middle name?"

"Bernadette."

"Oh! So your first name?—"

"Mary."

Elise gathered up the photographs and put them all back into the shoebox, except for the three she'd found of Michael taken during the years she was a Benedictine nun. In one, Michael stood alone in a black floor-length tunic next to a bank of pink azaleas in full bloom. Her eyes squinted in what looked like noontime sun and the snug white headdress she wore under her black veil made her face look like it was hanging in space. Elise supposed that Michael was twenty or twenty-one years old in the photo. She looked happy.

Elise found the red cotton sundress she'd worn to Michael's the day before on top of the dresser in the short narrow hall between the apartment's kitchen and bathroom. Michael had folded it into a crisp little square that Elise turned over and over in her hands before shaking it out and pulling it over her head. She left her sandals tucked under the dresser.

She'd sort of moved into the studio with Michael, and she also kept some of her stuff at her mother's house, but she spent most of her time at the house Carrie had recently bought with the settlement from her divorce. Elise felt most comfortable at Carrie's. They were both heartsore in their own way, so there was plenty to talk about, and they'd agreed to just let each other cry or throw a book at the wall or listen to every song on *Heart Like a Wheel* ten times in a row if that's what they needed to do.

When Elise let herself in, Carrie was lying on her couch watching a hummingbird graze the feeder she'd hung just outside the living room windows.

"Hey, babe," Carrie said.

"Hey, babe. You look like a babe. Are you going out?"

Carrie ran her hands over the skirt of the cream-colored silk dress she was wearing. "No, I just wanted to be fancy today."

Elise sat on the ottoman next to her sister. "Slam-dunk. You look great."

"Thanks." She rolled onto her side to face Elise. "How's your love triangle? Has that blown up in your face yet?"

"Not yet. I never hear from Jody anymore. I just have a feeling they're still carrying on."

"I know. You can carry on with whoever you want, then, right?"

Elise's eye caught the hummingbird. "Look at this guy." She lifted her chin in the direction of the windows. "I don't really feel like carrying on right now. I don't know."

"You're just growing up. It's good, Elise. You're thirty years old."

"I know how old I am, Carrie. I'm not done carrying on. I'm just thinking about other things."

Carrie got up and walked into the kitchen for a glass of water. She brought one to Elise, too, and they each lit a cigarette from a pack that Carrie pulled from under the couch.

"You don't have to hide those, Miss. This is your house."

"I'm embarrassed. It's so disgusting."

Elise took a deep drag and got up to open a window. "It's so delicious. You should call one of your exes and ask them to take you on a date tonight. You're all set."

"Not everybody does that, Elise. You're the only person I know with the nerve to do that."

"After some time passes it's so easy. So easy. You already

know each other's ways and at the end of the night you just peace out until whenever."

"I wish I could make myself not care what people think. I wish I could sleep around and be a wild ass."

"Then do it! Just start doing it. It's like wearing red lipstick. Start doing it and pretty soon people expect it. And it makes you feel sexy."

"It makes *you* feel sexy." Carrie pointed her cigarette at Elise.

"I always feel sexy," Elise shrugged. "Even when I'm all by myself." She put her open palm against the window pane.

She didn't have to explain things again. She'd already said everything she knew how to say. Elise and Jody met Michael at AA. They had the same home group, and the meetings were held three times a week at the Catholic church Elise and her sisters had grown up attending, Our Lady, Star-of-the-Sea. A couple of weeks after she managed to seduce Michael, Elise told Jody that she was leaving, and that's when she found out that Michael and Jody had been sleeping together for a year. But Michael wanted Elise and Elise loved the way that made her feel. High as a kite. She decided to keep seeing Michael. Then asked her sister to dinner one evening to hear her advice. Carrie had been appalled. "What are the odds that something like this would happen? *Mon Dieu*, love, what are y'all *doing* over there?"

"What are the odds? That three hot, dysfunctional lesbians would meet at a recovery meeting and start sleeping together? Ruining their relationships all around? The odds are really good, Carrie," Elise answered. "Like, really good."

"Who do you like the most?" Carrie asked.

"I like them both. For different reasons."

"Who do you love?"

"Jody? Jody, most of the time."

"Who makes more money?"

"Wow Carrie, no." Elise held up her hands.

"What?"

"Nothing, it doesn't matter. They're both broke."

"Of course they are."

"Stop being ugly. I don't care about that."

"She's older than you. A lot older."

She didn't necessarily regret telling her sister what happened, but she knew it wouldn't be much help. Carrie was crisp and practical and very spoiled. She was in her forties and still treated Elise like a baby sister. She thought of Elise as reckless and arrogant and very spoiled. Carrie loved her. She walked Elise to her car and placed foil-wrapped packages of leftovers on the passenger seat. She turned to Elise and brushed her long hair off her shoulders, then squeezed them. "Stay with me until you figure this out, my love. I'm nervous for you."

Elise could smell her perfume, white flowers and roses.

Carrie could see the bird hovering behind Elise's silhouette.

"Nervous about what?"

It was true: Michael was older than Elise. A lot older. Elise took her sister's hands in hers and swung them back and forth until she felt Carrie's arms go loose. "She's nice to me. She's good to me."

"Okay, baby." Carrie was always sweet to Elise, and on her side in most fights.

"I mean it."

"Alright, darling."

It was true: Michael was good to Elise. Once, when they were first getting into it, she'd told Michael that she had an *envie* for a piece of cold watermelon and Michael drove two hours to Opelousas and back with an ice chest in the back seat of her car so that Elise could have a ripe Sugartown watermelon and not one of the mealy bullshit ones from Wal Mart. Michael listened to Elise and offered to do things for her. Elise let her do lots of things for her: Run downtown and pay her parking tickets. Put gas in her car. Buy her cigarettes. Look through her mail for anything scary and sit with her while she handled it. Rub her back. Michael got really good at polishing Elise's nails and cleaning the gold hoop earrings and herringbone bracelet Elise wore every day. She got good at making hard scrambled eggs and washing complicated lingerie with Woolite in the sink.

Elise was, in return, an okay girlfriend. Sometimes she was very, very good: Planning the best birthday Michael ever had, a trip to Sedona to sit in the energy vortexes. Buying and decorating a seven-foot Christmas tree that took up a third of the space in Michael's apartment. Sending sweet cards. Sending nudes. Making lasagna from scratch whenever Michael asked. She called Michael ML, short for "my love," but not all the time. She liked to see Michael's face light up when she said it. Sometimes she was kind of the worst: Disappearing for days at a time, leaving Michael to drive by her mother's house or her sister's or the hair salon where Elise worked to make sure she was okay. Elise was fussy, and she fussed a lot when she didn't get her way. She liked to yell. She liked to bring up the fact that Michael had been sleeping with Jody before they got together, but what could she say? What else could she bear to hear?

Elise forgot to tell Michael she'd gone to Carrie's for the night. It was getting dark outside when Michael texted, trying to find her.

> Your sandals are here but I don't see *you*

> Oh! I'm at Carrie's. We're watching movies tonight so so so sorry

> What movies?

> Ann Reinking double feature. I need to be with Ann Reinking rn plz respect my privacy lol

> So, Annie?

> ofc

What's the other one? All that jazz?

No Micki & Maude!

That tiresome thing??

Hey don't yuck my yums. The clothes are cool

Ok. See you soon?

Tomorrow

Ok ilylyly

Mais oui

You're something else

MAIS OUI!

Carrie made grilled cheese sandwiches and they watched part of *Micki & Maude* together, and then decided they'd rather watch *Terms of Endearment* again. They'd watched it together at least ten times.

"Look at her eyeliner, damn. Her *nails*," Carrie said when the scene came on where Shirley MacLaine tells Debra Winger she's not special enough to overcome a bad marriage.

"I know. Hey. You're special enough to overcome a bad marriage."

Carrie pinched Elise's arm, "No shit. What are you going to do about your situation?"

"Nothing. I don't know." She shifted on the couch and picked up her phone. "What do you mean?"

"If you wanted to be with her, Elise, you would *be* with her. You wouldn't be in my spare bedroom three nights a week. I know you. You always rush in and move in and *merge*. Do you want Jody back?"

Elise could feel hot tears forming in her eyes. "No, and Jody doesn't want me either. I don't care about that. I can't make myself care about either of them right now, really."

Carrie turned to face Elise, "Let them go, then! Let them have each other, who gives a fuck? You can stay here as long as you want." She squeezed Elise into her side.

"I'm just not done with her."

"With Michael."

"Yes. It's not like that. It's a spiritual thing, it's—" Elise was crying hard now—"something else."

# VI

## THE APARTMENT SONG

*Get in the shower. Hurry up, she'll be here in a few minutes, and you want to catch her before she can knock on your door.*

*Say:* "Alexa, play 'Dancing in the Dark'".

*Wait, don't take a shower. If she says you smell good, it will make you weak. You're fine, you smell like yourself. You smell like the restaurant where you work. You smell like the Sunday brunch shift you just finished. Count your tips and listen for her car to pull up. Put all the twenties together, and the tens, and the fives, and then stuff the ones in the money-for-cigarettes jar on top of the refrigerator. Open the refrigerator door and close it. You're not hungry. Walk in a circle in your kitchen for a minute.*

*You know what? Call your Al-Anon sponsor right quick. Call JudgeJulie.*

*Flinch a little when she corrects you. Says:* "No? You're not stupid? Your choices are?"

*Fuck JudgeJulie for making everything she says sound like a question and then ask G_d to help you stop judging Julie and yourself. Don't think about Al-Anon, actually. Don't think about the last time you saw her at the noon meeting when she started talking about having a new qualifier and how that person's messiness was bringing up some control issues she was working to* surrender. *Don't think about how you had to sit on your hands and then put your fingers in your mouth so that you didn't shout: Look motherfucker, your new qualifier is my qualifier and if you think its bad now, wait until your new qualifier "borrows" one of the nice James Perse t-shirts* that you saved your tips for *and then spills the mango kombucha* that you saved your tips for *down the front and washes it in hot water without Spray and Wash so it gets fucking ruined, plus there was basically no kombucha left, just the gummy dregs and her backwash. Stop thinking about that and every other upsetting, messy thing Elise did when you were together. Answer the door. She's here, and that's what you get for thinking . . . for feeling . . . for re-feeling . . .*

*JudgeJulie says:* "Look at your own shit. Resentments? from the Latin: *Resentire,* to re-feel?"

*Let her kiss you. Let her kiss you on the lips really quickly and then on the space between your neck and collarbone a little longer because that makes you weak. Fuck it, just let yourself be weak. Right. Now stop her before she can get her hands further into the back pockets of your jeans.*

*Say:* "Michael, we talked about this."

*Think about the time you hooked up after the noon meeting, a different noon meeting, and you were both wearing black jeans and she accidentally wore yours home and you wore her jeans for the rest of the day and finally understood what people meant when they said that sometimes cheating is exciting.*

*Remember, Jody:* You were cheating, too. You were cheating first, remember?

*Okay, stop kicking yourself in the ass. You felt like shit most of the time. Remember that.*

*Say:* "Alexa, stop."

*It's time to go. Get your wallet and nudge her toward the door.*

*Buckle up. Reach for the radio and then put your hand back in your lap because its not like that anymore.*

*Look out the window when she says:* "Hey, that's okay."

*Plug the aux cord into your phone and play "No Surrender"*

*by Bruce Springsteen. Start talking about Bruce Springsteen. You both love Bruce Springsteen. See, this is easy. Everything is fine.*

Look *at her. She's looking at the road.* Look *at the veins on the back of her hands and the place on her neck where her silver hair tapers to a perfect V.* Look *at her thighs.* Feel *like reaching over and squeezing her knee and then leaving your hand there. It's not like that anymore.*

Feel that. Re-feel that.

*Throw some things into a basket at the store. You need tampons. You need dish soap. You need bread. Figure out pretty quickly that she's buying things for Elise: Oreos and grape jelly. Tampons, razors. Those nice expensive razors.*

Feel that.

*Start to wonder why you agreed to let her come and get you. Wonder why you're trying so hard to fit her into your life in some way, any way. Wonder why you're trying so hard. Wonder why you're trying.*

*Pay for your groceries and put them in the back seat of her car. Take her bags and put them next to yours. Tell yourself to stop being codependent, to let people put their groceries wherever they want.*

*Ask her to take you home. You don't want to run any more errands. Say you're tired. Say that brunch was busy. Play Tom Petty on the drive home. "The Apartment Song."*

*She can't stand the sound of his voice. Let her put her hand on your thigh and leave it there, even though it's not like that anymore.*

Look *out the window and think about the time Elise went shopping in New Orleans with her mother for the weekend and you spent the entire time in Michael's apartment. In her bed. In her bathtub.* Think *about the bruises her thumbs left on the insides of your thighs.*

Re-feel that.

*Jump out when she pulls into the space in front of your house. Duck into the backseat for your bags.*

Look *at her in the front seat.* Look *at her looking down into her lap behind the wheel, the reflection of her crown in the rearview mirror. She's looking at her phone.*

*Reach into her bag and shift the package of expensive razors into yours. Rustle the plastic and act busy while you grab her other bag, the one with Elise's Oreos and grape jelly. Put it down on the pavement and shift it back with your foot; make sure you wedge it tight in front of her back tire with your foot.*

*Now take her other bag and put it on the ground there too. Say: "*. . . bye, Sugar."

*Slam the door.*

Look away.

# VII

## THE RELIGIOUS LIFE

Elise spent a lot of time at the adoration chapel at the church where her AA meetings were held. Just beyond the door to the sanctuary, next to a row of confessionals, there was another door she'd passed at least a hundred times before entering. There was no handle, just a keypad, and when she typed in the code a section of the dark paneling clicked open. Behind it was a narrow room with three red velvet-covered kneelers and an altar with a gold monstrance holding the blessed Eucharist. A bank of tea lights stood to one side of the door, along with a table that held a box of matches and a cardboard box for donations. Next to the cardboard box was a laminated page of rules:

1. Cross yourself as soon as you walk through the door.

2. Never turn your back on the Eucharist.

3. Never leave Christ alone. If no one else is here when you need to leave, call the number to the rectory—it's posted by the light switch.

4. Don't tell anyone the door code (333).

5. Don't touch the thermostat.

Once she was in, Elise couldn't get out. This was starting to be a problem.

She was seventeen the first time she visited the chapel. She missed her period twice and told her mother that if she was pregnant she'd probably want to have the baby and raise it.

"Elise, I just finished paying for your prom dress. What about LSU?" Her mother asked. "You don't have to do that, baby. We can figure something out."

Elise and Carrie could never take their mother seriously because her devotion to Catholicism only extended to the limits of their menstrual cycles. Carrie had had an abortion in high school, expedited by their mother, also in the name of LSU. She wanted them all to go to college so badly. They went to college.

Their mother must have had an attack of conscience because she took Elise to the chapel to pray before the emergency appointment she'd made with her gynecologist for a test; the three-pack of EPTs God told her to buy from the drugstore instead had yielded one positive and two negatives. Elise wasn't pregnant.

The second time Elise went to the chapel was when she first got sober, just three months earlier. She'd accidentally overdosed on Xanax and Crown Royal one afternoon and ended up in the emergency room. It was the fourth time she'd been hospitalized, after bingeing on booze and pills, and she was burned out. She'd been partying for sixteen straight years by then and she couldn't do it anymore. Sure, she'd casually quit drinking or drugging—never both at the same time—once or twice before, but this was different. This time scared her. She was done. A couple of days later, Jody had taken her to an AA meeting and stopped drinking with her.

The beginning was the worst. One morning her cravings were so bad that she called her mother and asked her to pray for her or light a candle or something, and her mother had come right over and taken her to the chapel. They sat in front of the exposed Eucharist for an hour and her mother held her hand while she cried, and then she dug a roll of cherry Lifesavers out of her purse. Elise ate six of them, one right after the other.

Sugar helped.

When they left that day Elise felt different, and she made it through the day sober. She began stopping there on the way to the meeting a couple of times a week to pray for a minute. After a couple of weeks it was like her feet automatically walked her there, even if she was running late and knew she'd miss part of the meeting. One evening she stayed for a few minutes longer because she wanted to, and the next evening she went back for an hour, even though there was no meeting. She told Jody she'd been reading magazines at the bookstore, and then wondered why she felt like she needed to lie.

She'd met Michael because of the chapel. Elise had stopped in the church's kitchen for a snack between the chapel and the meeting and Michael was there, making sandwiches for the district picnic. They started sitting together at the meeting, and then going for coffee afterward. They were attracted to one another, but for different reasons. Michael like Elise's humor and her boldness. She liked the fact that Elise had a lot of energy. She liked Elise's face and she really liked her body. Michael's body reminded Elise of Jody's, in a way—long and rangy and hard. Muscles and bones and light as a feather. Michael's body was thirty-three years older than Jody's, and Elise expected this to be an obstacle in their sex life for some reason she couldn't quite name, but no. No. She really liked Michael's body and the fact that Michael knew how to do things with it that Elise hadn't even had a chance to think of yet.

The biggest draw for Elise, though, was learning that Michael had been a nun in her twenties, part of an order of cloistered Dominican nuns who dedicated their lives to prayer and meditation. It was a detail Michael shared early in their friendship, and it solidified Elise's feeling that meeting Michael *meant* something. She needed it to be cosmic.

A week earlier, she'd been in the chapel at the same time as the church's secretary, a woman named Jeanne who'd known Elise since she was a baby. Elise could feel Jeanne's eyes on her a couple of times, but she kept her gaze fixed on the host. She didn't have anything against Jeanne, really; she just wanted to be left alone.

*Maybe Jeanne saw me chewing gum,* she thought. *Fuck. If she gives me a hard time, I'll just make myself cry. I can do that.* And then Jeanne was there at her side, sliding into the bench. *Dammit, fuck, fuck, Jeanne can't you see I'm praying?*

"Hi, Jeanne," she whispered.

"Elise, listen," she put her hand on Elise's arm and looked into her eyes with an intensity that Elise did not like at all. "When I saw you come in I said a little prayer for you and I got a message."

"Okay." *Oh, boy.*

"I got a message to come over here and ask you if you've ever considered the religious life. Those were the exact words," she made air quotes with her fingers, "the religious life."

Elise felt her scalp and her face tingle, and goosebumps sprung up on her arms, "Jeanne," she said, squeezing Jeanne's hand on her forearm, "you've known me since the day I was born. Does that make sense?"

"No, but—"

"Come on, now. What kind of sense does that make?"

Jeanne stood up and patted Elise's bare shoulder, "I know, but it's what I heard. You need to cover up your arms in here, sweet."

Elise rolled her eyes and cracked her gum. She pulled down the kneeler, "Next time. Bye, Jeanne." She hit her knees and put her forehead into her folded hands.

Elise was haunted by what Jeanne said because her time at the chapel had started getting weird. The AC blew cold air into the tiny space all day and night, from what she could tell, but a particular energy filled the space and made it feel, if not warm, enervated and alive. She was never alone there, and she and some of the people she saw regularly began to acknowledge each other with a nod. Once, a woman who looked about her mother's age waved a hand at Elise's bare knees with a gesture that meant she should cover them up, and Elise mouthed to her what she'd said to Jeanne: *Next time*.

She kept showing up in whatever she'd been wearing that day. A sundress or shorts and a t-shirt. Once, a pair of cutoff overalls with a pink bikini top underneath. No one else said anything.

She'd bless herself with holy water from the font in the sanctuary before she entered the chapel, and then pray on her knees for a few minutes once she was inside, out of habit more than anything. She'd been pulling the kneeler down and cranking out a couple of Hail Marys whenever she arrived at church since her First Holy Communion in second grade. As soon as she settled into the pew, it was on. She lifted her eyes to the host in the monstrance and then it was all she could see.

At first, she assumed that the hum of the air conditioner and the heavy smell of wax rolling off the never-not-burning cluster of tall ivory candles on the altar was making her sleepy or allergic, lulling her into a weird passivity she didn't exactly mind, but what was happening didn't originate in her sinuses or bronchial tract. She knew what drugs felt like. It was happening in her brain and it felt just like drugs.

"Do you ever go into trance at church?" she asked Michael one evening after the meeting.

"I don't go to church anymore."

"Did you ever?"

"Go to church or into a trance?"

"Come on," Elise nudged Michael's side with her elbow. "I'm trying to talk to you here. Into a trance."

"No."

Elise had begun to tell Michael about what she was

experiencing in the chapel more than once, but she was distracted by the sex they'd been having and didn't want that heat to go away.

She also told her sister Carrie, but that hadn't gone very well. Carrie thought she was joking when she mentioned what Jeanne had said to her about the religious life, when she admitted that the comment had been following her around, driving her nuts.

"Elise. Are you feverish?" She pressed Elise's forehead with her palm, and then put her cheek next to Elise's cheek. "Since when do you love . . . The Lord?"

Carrie had a point.

"Fair. That's not who I'm seeing in there, though. It's not a Jesus thing."

It wasn't a Jesus thing. It wasn't someone she recognized, more like a pastiche of a few someone's: virgins and martyrs she'd learned about in catechism and maybe Sissy Spacek in *Carrie* a little bit, and an amalgamation of the Lisbon sisters (all five) in *The Virgin Suicides*—Elise loved that book. These are the compartments she established in her mind to help her make sense of the image that pulled her into the pew, onto her knees in the chapel.

It started after the cherry LifeSavers visit with her mother. She was there on a Wednesday before the meeting and there were a few other people around, an elderly couple and a woman about Elise's age who wore a chapel veil over her long mousey hair. Elise settled into the pew and checked her text messages. She hadn't taken her headphones off when she entered, and "Take Me with U" by Prince was playing, and then "Nothing Compares 2 U" came on. She felt her eyes relax as she looked at the host, the edges of the monstrance going blurry. When the part of the song where Prince says he could put his arms around every girl he sees came on, Elise saw the host rupture and crack open. White light spilled out and she could feel it, a pressure in her chest that made her want to take a deep breath. The light blew the whole room open and the people and the candles and the kneelers went away. She was there alone in the light, with the Eucharist yawning open, and the only sound was the sound of Prince's voice in her headphones. She looked into her lap to refocus her eyes, and when she looked up, the lady was there. It was as if she'd hatched from an egg but the egg was the monstrance and she balanced herself at the edge.

At first, Elise thought she was seeing the Virgin Mary, but this lady did not fit the description of any of the iterations familiar to Elise: Guadalupe, Mt. Carmel, Lourdes. Her robe was dove gray and soaking wet; the fabric clung to her skin and she shivered in the light. Her long hair was wet and tangled under a golden crown floating just above her head. Bloody tears had dried on her face, and as she reached for Elise, a tiny dove flapped from each of her palms. When she opened her mouth to speak, red and yellow rose petals fell from her mouth, landing in a pile that covered her bare feet. When Elise opened her own mouth to speak, the host began to close. The light faded. The lady was drawn back into the monstrance, and she was in the room again with the elderly couple and the woman who wore a chapel veil over her long mousey hair.

"Hey, do you ever get flashbacks from when we partied in college?" Elise was in her car in the parking lot, talking to her college boyfriend, Tyler.

"I don't know, girl. Those LSU memories are so hazy. How's my girl? When are you coming to see me?" Tyler was all grown-up now. He played golf and owned a State Farm agency in Shreveport.

"I don't know how your girl is. You tell me. How *is* Holly? How's that baby?"

"Look—"

"And I'm not talking about memories, I mean like flashbacks. Like, sometimes I see tracers when the sun is really bright."

"Yeah, but you really liked acid, Li. I didn't do that too much."

"But doesn't ecstasy stay in your spinal cord, in the fluid?"

"Sweetheart, don't tell me that. Holly wants to have another baby soon. That's gonna stress me out."

"Tyler."

She went home and googled:

- acid flashbacks
- symptoms of alcohol withdrawal
- hallucinations from sobriety
- religious visions
- Prince religious visions
- ecstasy in spinal fluid

It kept happening. Elise returned to the chapel again and again, waiting for the lady to reappear; and she did. Elise knew she was supposed to be working on her relationship with her Higher Power, and had begun to think that maybe this was it. As repulsive and terrifying as the image had seemed at first, she was interested in what was happening in her mind or her soul that could make such a vision re-appear, and she felt close to knowing her creator, for the first time ever.

Early in her sobriety she'd had a talk with Jody one night while they cooked dinner together, about who they each believed their personal higher powers might be.

Jody had nothing. Elise was committed to the idea of the natural world as an expression of God. She'd grown up Catholic and was still haunted by the crucifix that hung over the blackboard in her first-grade classroom.

"It was made of unpainted porcelain, and even the figure of Christ in His Exquisite Agony was bone white," Elise said. She'd taken one look at it on the first day of school and burst into tears. She cried until she threw up, and Carrie had to be called from her high school classroom in the building next door to walk her home.

"The entire school year was like this. Crying and throwing up and nightmares, too." She had never seen a nearly naked man before. She had never seen a man in pain. She had never known that cheating on a spelling test or lying to her mother could cause a nearly naked man to experience even more pain. "'It makes Jesus and His Blessed Mother cry, *don't you know that*,' was the way the nun who taught my first-grade class said it. After that: Flowers, honeybees, crashing waves? Expressions of God. No more men."

No more people, until now. She wished she could talk to Jody again. The lady she'd been seeing grossed her out and made her question her sanity. The lady excited Elise and fascinated her, too. It was a lot.

Apart from that, she looked forward to the dreamy, druggy feeling that fell on her like an avalanche when she entered the chapel, a feeling that lasted into the evening and the next day sometimes. The thing that worried her was that she did not feel worried at all, or afraid. She knew that she should probably be afraid of what was happening. Of course, she didn't love the way the lady followed her home sometimes. Elise wanted their communication to stay inside the walls of the chapel or at least the walls of the church. She wanted to go home and cook dinner and take a bath and not think of bloody tears streaming from pleading eyes, not think about the reason the lady was soaking wet and shivering each time she appeared.

Finally, one day, Elise was brushing the tangles out of her own long hair after she'd washed it and as she attacked a wet knot with her comb she flashed on the lady's face, silently watching, and it pissed her off. She slapped the comb against the side of the sink.

*What is your name?* she asked, exasperated. The comb fell to the floor. Elise bent down to grab it.

The lady disappeared.

At the chapel the next day, Elise sat down and closed her eyes for a few minutes and asked again, nicer.

*I need to call you something. What should I call you?*

No answer, but the lady was there, and she looked different. More serene. It took a minute for Elise to notice that her cheeks were clean. No bloody tear stains. The lady stepped off the monstrance onto the altar.

Elise pulled the kneeler down.

The lady disappeared.

The tension of her spiritual secret—wanting to know, not wanting to know—was wearing her out. She had no patience for anything but her pursuit to decode the situation she was beginning to suspect she had conjured with her imagination. *Was* it a drug flashback? Guilt? Some kind of growing pains she'd have to endure until she could graduate to a Higher Power who was just a little less *extra*?

Her relationship with Michael was still clicking along because Michael was careful with her and made sure she had what she wanted. Sometimes this reminded Elise of living with Jody and she wondered what it would be like if she just pushed Michael in Jody's direction and called it good. Would they cancel each other out with all their attention and care?

The more Elise thought about having a religious life, the less she wanted to be someone's girlfriend, which is not to say she wanted to give up the things she liked and knew she was good at. Taking long baths. Putting on makeup. Cooking when she felt like it. Running and driving and listening to music and especially having sex. She wanted to keep all of that. That part of her relationship with Michael still worked, though they were seldom alone in bed together. Crowding between them, next to the specter of Jody: The lady. Elise had gotten better at blocking thoughts of Jody during sex, but the lady was more insistent, and more upsetting.

One Monday morning, Michael woke up early to get Elise

kombucha and a latte for breakfast. When she got home, she woke Elise and they lay in bed together for a long time talking and kissing. Elise was naked and Michael was wearing the jeans and flannel she'd put on to run errands, which felt cozy and hot at the same time to Elise.

"Take this off? Take this off," she pulled on the collar of the flannel.

They were still getting to know each other in bed. That day, Elise didn't want to be on top, and then she didn't like it on her back.

"Am I not in the right place?"

"No, this is good, I'm just concentrating."

"Should I—"

"Keep going, I'm getting into it." She wasn't. Every time she closed her eyes and tried to enjoy the feeling of Michael's hands all over her, her fingers inside of her, the lady was there with her wet robe and pleading, bloody eyes. Elise was about to give up—get up and have another coffee and a bath—when she remembered how to make the lady go away. She opened her eyes and squeezed Michael's shoulder, "Hang on, love—I just need to get on my knees."

# VIII

## CARDIO ANNIHILATION

*You can't exercise it off.*

*You've tried, but your body just won't do the things it used to, like consume breakfast sandwiches from Starbucks and hot pita bread with butter and olives, and Rice Krispy treats studded with chocolate chips and spread with sugary peanut butter without a problem. The problem? Your puffy cheeks and tummy, the new pads of fat that push against the sides of your jeans.*

*You stop eating sugar but crave the two berry-flavored acidophilus tabs and chewy antacids you take with your morning coffee, shaking the container until a pink and a yellow fall out.*

*You are interested in exercise for the first time ever though, exercise that isn't part of some natural movement like working retail or going on the occasional hike. You bought a subscription to an app that offers daily workouts that kick your ass. Led by beautiful people in their twenties, the classes are intense, full body hit-and-runs of cardio, weights, and stretching that leave you wrung out. You sleep so deeply that you wake up with a headache, the covers around you completely undisturbed.*

*Log in and scroll through a list of choices. You press play on:*

"45-Minute Cardio Annihilation with Angela."

*Angela is wearing a purple tank top and matching leggings with bright white sneakers. You are wearing a white undershirt and pair of black leggings from Lululemon that your ex left at your apartment when she moved out. Not really left, she forgot them in the dryer, along with some of her other gear, a black sports bra that fits you so tightly it takes your breath away, and a pair of bike shorts in a bright blue leopard pattern.*

*Angela sweeps her arms up and over her head and you take a sip of water and wait for her to get serious.*

Let any stress, any tension just fall away.

*When Angela tells you to get in a plank on your elbows, you do it. When she tells you to focus on a spot on the floor in front of you or close your eyes and think of something besides nailing your belly button to your spine and squeezing your glutes, allow yourself to think of the woman your girlfriend left you for, but only for one minute.*

So when you wanna drop, don't do it. You can handle it.

*This woman is the only thing you have in common now. Elise forwarded her mail and the bills were in your name, so. The day she moved out, you went through the refrigerator and threw away her half-consumed jars of pickles (dill and spicy), crusty bottles of salad dressing, and the tub of miso she used to make soup for three days after she read* The Macrobiotic Way *and then abandoned it.*

Hold it back.

*Think about what they're probably doing right now. Its 7 am so Elise is asleep. Michael is drinking coffee maybe, or taking a bath. She likes to wake up early. You know this because she called you early in the morning when she was chasing you. She knew you'd be up, too. You let her catch you a couple of times.*

For four, for three, for two . . .

*She still calls you, but only to talk about Elise.*

We'll put it together.

*The differences between you and Elise.*

It's . . . reach . . . out.

*Michael says she misses you, and it bothers her that Elise says she misses you and it bothers Elise that Michael says out loud to her that she misses you. It's all out in the open now and now they both miss you.*

Good. Keep it up.

*Angela wants to do jumping jacks now, so you do jumping-jacks with Angela.*

I don't know about you . . .

*Mountain climbers. Back on the floor.*

Two . . . Last one.

*Wipe your hands and your face on your tank top and pull up Spotify on your computer. You can't listen to electronic dance music anymore. Shuffle the first playlist and press play.* Neutral Milk Hotel: *no.* Mary Lou Lord: *no.* Yaz: *okay. Electronic dance music competes with the sound of Angela's voice.*

Out . . . Out.

*Angela is really trying to annihilate you now. More jumping jacks. She tells you to think about*

. . . how you want to feel at the end of class. Halfway there. Two more. Last one.

*You want to* feel *less fucked up about the end of your relationship. You want to stop missing Michael. You want to* feel *her hands on your body again. You want to feel* like she wants to put her hands on only you. *Angel Olson: yes. It's less about how you* feel, *and more about what you know. You know what she does to Elise because she tells you.*
*You say,* I did that with her, too.
Not the way that I do it, *she says, and you know she's right because she did it with you, too, and you want to do it again.*
*Stop thinking about their bodies. Think about your body.*

Maybe you just dance it out. Just smile.

*You danced for a couple of months in your twenties, an endeavor that left your calves and shoulders contracted and achy, but was energizing in its own way.*
*Apart from drugs and alcohol, money and attention were your central obsessions, and the job provided a glut of it all. Dave, your cute funny boss at the club was in his thirties and crushed on you a little. He looked like Dave Holmes on MTV, and you called him Dave Holmes to his face. One word: Daveholmes. He fired you after you came to work hungover and fought with another girl in the dressing room. She'd taken a sip of your shift drink, a double-well gin, so you snatched the chain she was wearing and shoved her to the ground. You spent the night in jail. That was eleven years ago.*
*Dancing was exercise, you supposed.*

Out and back, good . . .

*Body image has never been a problem for you until now. You sprouted up quick, 5'11" in seventh grade, and your weight never quite caught up. The way you've changed these last few months upsets you, but it's fascinating, too. You never really had hips before, and you like the way they look when you're naked, but it freaks you out to see the way you look in jeans. Curvy, not straight up and down.*

Carve it out, up and down.

*Stop thinking about how your straight-up-and-down body fit perfectly into the bathtub in Michael's apartment next to her straight-up-and-down body. The bathtub she's probably sitting in right now, smoking a cigarette.* Mitski: yes. *It's Tuesday, the day you'd both be at the noon Al-Anon meeting. After the meeting, you'd somehow end up back at your place or her place, tearing each other apart and smoking cigarettes and talking. Every Tuesday you'd promise it was the last time you'd do that and then she'd send you a text a few hours later, something dirty and exciting about the way you taste or the sounds you make when you come.*

Over, under, there it is.

*Don't go to Al-Anon. Text her and tell her you need to go to Al-Anon and she should stay away. Text your Al-Anon sponsor and tell her you've been having an affair with a woman she introduced you to at Al-Anon. Do neither of those things. Do a dozen jump squats with Angela.*

Carve it out, carve it out. Yes, out, out.

*The person you don't want to talk to is Elise, but it bothers you that she never texts or calls.*

Like a really. big. reach.

## ENUMERATE THE WAYS SHE HURT YOU AND DROVE YOU CRAZY SO THAT THE SILENCE FEELS LIKE WHAT YOU NEED.

1. *Elise is messy: She can't even fold her own clothes. She's always had someone to do that for her. Her mother, her sister, then you. Michael must be doing that for her now. You'd bet money on it.*

2. *Elise is messy: She ran off your best friends with her comments about their jobs and girlfriends and now you have to promise them you won't take her back (again) before they'll hang out with you.*

3. *Elise is messy: She's cheated before, with the guy she works for, a middle-aged, playboy hairdresser from New Orleans who you actually sort of like. He's charming and you can see why she let him seduce her. You might actually enjoy sleeping with him, too.*

Little, little, big.

4. *Elise is messy: She won't introduce you to her homophobic mother but insists that you drop her off over there every Sunday for dinner, even though she has her own car and can take herself.*

5. *Elise is messy: Each week, she asks you to make cookies or brownies or banana bread to bring to Sunday dinner at her mother's house.*

Two. Last one.

6. *Elise is messy.*

Up front. Up back. Get low.

## REMEMBER THE FUCKED-UP WAY YOU ACTED. THINK ABOUT THE REASONS YOU ACTED THAT WAY.

Pulse, pulse. pulse.

*You cheated, too, for a long time. You lied.*

Are you warmed up?

*At first, you were so overwhelmed with guilt that you could barely eat or sleep. Instead of eating and sleeping, you thought about Michael. Kissing Michael. Talking to her. Having sex. While you were kissing, talking to, having sex with Elise: Michael, Michael, Michael.*

Shake it off, shake it off.

*You loved her. You fell in love.*

One more slow.

*Elise noticed that you were distracted, but you played it off as anxiety about staying sober and doubled down on meetings. That was easy.*

Twist. Really twist!

*You could see her four or five times a week that way. She'd sit a row or two behind you and you could feel her eyes on your neck, the back of your head.*

Push yourself. Get out of your comfort zone, right?

*You'd show up last minute and slide into the seat next to her,
something she'd asked you to do, and then told you never to do.*

I want that heart rate to get up.

*She said that the way you touched her hand when you passed
the basket made her weak. She said that the smell of the pomade
you use in your hair made her mouth water. She told you to stop.*

You got eight, seven, really squeeze it.

*You'd stop for a couple of meetings and then do it again. Those
were the days you were really on fire, both of you.*

One more slow. Now make it more fluid.

*The thing that messes with you now is the way that fire never
waned. When you did the math, you realize that the entire time she
was seducing Elise, she was right there with you, stronger than ever.
Texts all day, little gifts, hot sex. Love. She said she loved you too.*

Stay low now. Out low. Out low.
It's like the ceiling lowered right above your head and you
can't stand up. Out, up.

*You loved Elise. You did. The life you made with her felt solid,
finally, and you had a routine. You went to bed at the same time
every night and changed the sheets together every Sunday. She
wasn't selfish all the time. Once, she came home from Whole Foods
with ten containers of the expensive yogurt you liked but felt guilty
for buying. You freaked out when you saw them lined up in the
fridge, reminding her that bills were due and you couldn't cover
her part. She'd gotten a big tip at work that day, and she wanted
to get you something. Something just for you.*

We're almost there.

*You had fun together in bed. Your energies matched.*

Twist.

*She made you laugh every day.*

Find a squat.

*Her natural smell: lemon and dust.*

Last one.

*Her body.*

Stay as low as you can.

*Her mind. She reads in the bathtub and taped poems from* The New Yorker *next to the mirror.*

Almost. done.

# IX

## HAND TO MOUTH

Jody spent a solid ten minutes every Friday night organizing her supplements and medication into a white plastic box divided into seven sections. She'd spent months searching for the perfect pill box but found the price of this one—$5.99— daunting. She took a picture of it and searched it on Amazon where it was a dollar cheaper but the tax and shipping made it closer to $7.00 and those calculations made her feel suddenly disgusted with herself so she drove to Whole Foods and bought the pill box and a couple of kombuchas plus a candy bar that cost more than the pill box. She ate the candy bar in her car, slowly, before going home and cleaning her new excellent pill box with 409 and a paper towel. She took down the bottles of supplements and medicine: vitamin B, vitamin C, Wellbutrin, Effexor, Nexium, turmeric, digestive enzymes. Clicking open the separate compartments, she loaded them in one at a time. She placed a bottle of iron tablets and prenatal vitamins off to the side because she took those alone, at night, when she remembered, because they upset her stomach.

After that, Jody started eating. She turned the broiler on and placed two slices of bread on a pan and covered each with butter and a slice of cheese. She poured a glass of vanilla soy milk and squeezed in a glob of honey. Downed it. Poured another, this time with cinnamon sprinkled on top. There were a couple of apples in the refrigerator, so she cut one up and scooped into the jar of crunchy peanut butter she kept in the door. Her ex-girlfriend Elise hated cold peanut butter, so Jody bought her a jar of her own to keep in the pantry.

The broiler started smoking, and she reached in and dragged the pan onto the top of the stove. The edges of the bread had blackened, but she could see that the cheese had browned perfectly, and that the center of the bread would still be soft and pillow-y. *Like biting a cotton ball*, she thought.

Jody exercised every day, but on Saturdays she doubled up and exercised herself to death, doing an hour of cardio on a stationary bike and then taking a hot yoga class at the gym near her house. Sometimes she ran on a treadmill or outside, but no matter what, she looked forward to dragging her sweaty, already-sore body home before noon to shower, eat a peanut butter and jelly sandwich, and then take a long nap. One Saturday, she noticed she'd parked crooked when she'd arrived at the gym, so she got back into her car to move it. The battery was dead. She cranked the key a few more times and then walked inside and got on a stationary bike. She thought about calling someone to come and get her but she didn't want to talk to anyone so she walked home.

Who would she call, anyway? Her parents lived in Biloxi and her friends were treating her like glass because her heart was broken, which got on her nerves. Calling Elise was out of the question. Doing that would lead to fighting or sex or fighting and sex and she was trying to take a tolerance break. It wasn't exciting anymore, just painful.

There was one person, she remembered, while she was taking a shower. There was a woman she'd taken on two dates but never kissed. Jamie was the woman's name, and she was definitely not Jody's type. They looked exactly alike: five ten and lanky, with black hair cut in a quiff. Soft butch tomboys with tan lines on their biceps and outlines of their wallets on the back pockets of their jeans.

"She's got these big, sexy, rough hands," she had explained to her friend Oliver over drinks one Friday night. "She works on campus in the Ag school."

"Doing what?" Oliver stirred his vodka soda with a cocktail straw. "Bailing hay? Feeding calves with those humongous baby bottles?"

"The books," Jody answered. "She's an accountant."

"Oh," Oliver said, looking deflated.

Jamie had an office job, it was true, but she still looked the Ag school part, wearing jeans and Carhartt henleys to work. The thing that she didn't tell Oliver was that Jamie hadn't put those big, sexy, rough hands on her yet, not really. "I should stop all this. I'm supposed to be doing something else."

"Someone else?" Oliver took a little sip of his drink through the skinny black straw.

"No, bitch. I need something more. I think I need something I can't get from another person."

"That's cute. That sounds cozy."

"You're a dick, my man. I'm trying to improve myself over here," she laughed.

"I know. I know you do your therapy worksheets."

"Fuck you."

"You go, girl. You go, boss bitch. I mean girlboss. You don't need a pair of rough hands for nothing."

"I'm leaving."

"Do some yoga." Oliver downed the rest of his drink and flagged the bartender. Jody ordered another Diet Coke to go and put a folded ten in the tip jar.

Jamie was at Jody's house to pick her up within the hour. She drove Jody to her car and gave it a jump and then asked Jody if she was busy that afternoon. "I'll take you to a movie. Or we can get ice cream."

"I want that."

"Which?"

"Ice cream."

Jody insisted on paying, and they both ordered a double scoop of cookies and cream. "I know you want to be like me." Jamie raised an eyebrow.

"I think we're a lot alike already," Jody answered.

They finally kissed that afternoon on the back porch at Jody's house. She'd invited Jamie over to watch a documentary about Isaac Mizrahi on Prime, and they'd sat politely on opposite ends of the couch together, drinking iced tea. At one point, Jody went to the kitchen and rinsed a couple of bunches of green grapes for a snack. She wrapped the colander in a towel and placed it on the couch between them and their hands brushed occasionally when they reached in. One of the times this happened, Jamie hooked her index finger over Jody's and pulled it toward her. She lifted Jody's hand out of the colander, to her lips, never taking her eyes off the television. Jody felt her face flush and her nipples get hard.

When the documentary ended, they sat on Jody's back porch and lighted cigarettes. It started to rain, and Jody rested her cigarette on the edge of the porch and ran into the yard to rescue a papier-mâché project she was working on for a class, a five-foot tall peace crane she'd painted white with pale blue stripes to resemble loose-leaf notebook paper. Jamie helped her drag the whole thing onto the porch and blotted the base with a dish towel while Jody patched a couple of soggy spots that were threatening to cave in. "What class is this for?"

"Paper Sculpture."

"Grad."

"Yeah, I'm almost done. How's Ag?"

"Ag is okay. Actually something amazing happened yesterday."

"Oh, cool." Jody picked up her cigarette and moved closer to Jamie.

"Mmmhm. I sent around a form for some profs and the Chair to sign and send to the dean and they did it."

"Okay."

"No, they just did it. All in one day."

"Right, so—"

"No, that's a big deal. That feels like a miracle." Jamie straightened up so that she and Jody were eye to eye.

"So the bar in Ag is really low," she tilted her chin and exhaled a plume of smoke at the ceiling.

Jamie reached for Jody's waistband and pulled her closer. She held Jody by the waist with her thumbs on Jody's hip bones and kissed her.

Jody didn't know where to put her hands. She was the one who reached for a belt buckle, or hipbones. She was the one whose hands knew their way around a waistline, who knew exactly where to rest her thumbs— ribcage, underwire, tip of the sternum. She finally rested her palms on Jamie's shoulders and leaned closer, returning her kiss with some intensity, some muscle.

Jamie wasn't having that. She drew back and looked Jody in the eyes. She gave Jody's hips a squeeze, "I'm driving," she said, kissing Jody's jawline and her neck.

Jody flicked her cigarette into the yard and moved her hands to Jamie's hips, sliding them into the back pockets of her jeans. She took Jamie's earlobe between her teeth, "I'm driving."

Jody sent Jamie home after fifteen minutes of vigorous kissing, promising to call. The next morning when she stepped outside to collect the newspaper, she found a glass jar full of daisies, a fresh pack of cigarettes, and a peace crane fashioned from loose-leaf notebook paper on the doormat. Written in red ink on the crane's wing: can I see u 2nite?

She took a picture of the pile of surprises and sent it to Oliver. *I can't I can't I can't do this right??*

She texted the same picture to Jamie. *Of course. Come over at 6? Come over now if you want :)))*

She took all of her meds and supplements with a glass of hot tap water. While she waited for the coffee finish brewing, she stood at her kitchen counter and unraveled the peace crane Jamie had made for her and folded it back more precisely. The red ink disappeared over the side of the wing. She unraveled it again and re-folded it along the original lines. It was kind of sloppy compared to the ones she made, but she let it be sloppy. Let it be the crane Jamie had made for her with her own two hands. She took a piece of junk mail lying on top of the recycling bin in the kitchen and folded it into a new crane—sharp, tiny, perfect.

She'd learned how to make the cranes from a YouTube video a couple of months before after her Judith, her therapist, recommended she find new ways to deal with her stress. "It should be something you're just average at. Don't try to master it, just keep the stakes low."

"I guess I could join the gay intramural soccer team."

"Jody, that's the same as what you're doing now."

"How?"

"Running. Exercise? Competition. Do you think you won't want to excel at that if you start?"

"Oh." They decided that Jody would start with one thing she was curious about but didn't feel like she'd get intense and uptight about: origami.

She mastered the peace crane after five or six tries, and then started making them out of any paper she could find that would fold. She made some from aluminum foil. From wax paper. From pages of cookbooks she bought at a library sale for a dollar apiece. She built a long, flat bin from plywood and painted it white and threw the cranes in as she made them. She couldn't just throw them away, and they'd begun to cover most of the flat surfaces in her house. She stored the bin on the bottom shelf of her pantry, next to the cans of soup and extra cases of LaCroix.

When Judith asked, Jody told her she'd abandoned origami for crosswords and that she was just okay at those. She couldn't tell her about the five hundred or so cranes she'd collected, much less her project, which she'd named Maximum-Strength Crane. She knew Judith would fuss. Jody just didn't want to be average at anything.

Jamie did come right over. Jody answered the door in the

boxers and t-shirt she slept in and Jamie stepped back, surprised. "Oh hey, I'm sorry. I didn't know you weren't ready."

"Ready for what? Come in, I have coffee." Jamie stood in the front hall while Jody went into the kitchen for coffee. She remembered, from one of their dates, that Jamie liked cream in her coffee, but all she had was oat milk. She heated a little in the cup in the microwave and poured the coffee on top. "Here, come on in."

Jamie took the cup but didn't move to follow Jody into the living room. "Why don't we go into the city? We can be there by lunch time and spend the afternoon."

"I need to work on my project. I'll make brunch, though."

"What if I get you back here by five?"

"Alright." Jody washed her face and stood in front of her closet. She put on a black bra and a white tank top and cutoffs. She put on some mascara and a squirt of Rose 31 and walked back into the kitchen. "Do you want a popsicle for the road?" She opened the freezer, "I have grape and red."

"Red?

"Yeah."

"Red isn't a flavor."

"It is."

"What does the box say?' Jamie walked into the kitchen.

"Cherry, but what kind of cherry tastes like this? Here, just take a grape, mercy," she handed the popsicle to Jamie.

"Why don't you put on something nice? I want to take you somewhere nice."

Jody laid her popsicle on the counter and took a sip from the cup of coffee she'd left there. "What?"

"Put on something pretty. You smell amazing." Jamie put her arms around Jody's waist.

"Let me see what I have." Jody went to her room and closed the door, and then she stood in her closet and closed that door, too. She called Oliver and told him what Jamie said.

"Doesn't she know you? What do you have on now?"

"Hang on," Jody took a selfie and sent it to Oliver.

"Oh, alright, Madonna. I like that black bra situation, that's hot. That's perfect, what you're wearing. I mean damn, it's just an afternoon in New Orleans." Jody heard someone talking in the background. "Kelly's still here," Oliver said. "Okay, Kelly said she'll bring you a dress."

"Oh, Kelly. Kelly's so pretty. I didn't know she was there."

"Yeah, so let's wrap this up. I think you should wear that ho pride Madonna outfit. Fuck a dress, dude, that's not you. She needs to take you as-is."

"I know. Okay."

"Kelly said she celebrates you. She sends a kiss to you."

"Tell Kelly to call me."

"Bye, bitch."

Jamie looked surprised when she walked back into the living room in her cutoffs. "I'm going to stay here and work on my project, I think. We can go to the city another time, maybe."

"I'll help you. What do you need to do?" Jamie stood up and Jody moved toward the front door.

She opened it.

# THANKS, BISCUIT

Elise had close to six months of sobriety. She texted Helen a week before the actual date and said that, "Higher Power willing," she'd be collecting her chip at her home group the next Thursday and asked if Helen would be there to do the honors. It had occurred to Elise that Helen wouldn't just say yes; that she'd want to see Elise and talk to her first, so in a fit of nerves and guilt, she added that she'd like to return to her neglected step work and finally make some amends.

Helen responded.

> I can meet with you on Tuesday at 7 am

*OK!* Elise wrote, then deleted the exclamation point and cringed, vowing never to avoid her sponsor for this long again. Each time she disappeared they had to start all over, and it took weeks for her to feel comfortable talking to Helen about her character defects and messed-up ways. Her alcoholism. She sent the text.

Helen texted back.

Great, I'll see you on Tuesday

"Higher Power willing" :)

When Tuesday came, Elise seriously considered texting Helen to say that she had woken up with a rash or a stomach bug (something contagious) and that she'd need to reschedule (which she might do at some point, but didn't want to think about right then), but she'd gotten to a place in sobriety where even little white lies felt uncomfortable, and she'd begun to doubt her ability to casually deceive people at all. The week before, her mother had asked Elise to run to the post office for stamps and Elise had *ummmmd* and *uhhhed* so much, searching for a believable excuse, that her mother finally shoved a twenty into her hand and thanked her. *I reckon I'm changing*, she thought that day. She'd always been able to summon a lie—lightning fast.

Elise and Helen had been meeting at a coffee shop to talk about recovery and step work each week until Elise disappeared after working Step Eight. The list of people she'd harmed was so varied and extensive that composing it had made her feel exhausted and anxious, and she wondered what kind of harm some of them might want to do to her if she contacted them to offer an amends. Some of the people had moved away. Her grandparents (all four) and her father had died in the early years of her active addiction, so she'd never have a chance to apologize to them for raiding their wallets and liquor cabinets and then lying to their faces about it. A few people had let her know, in no uncertain terms, that they'd like to forget ever making her acquaintance at all. The eighth step had really kicked her ass.

When Elise walked through the door that morning, Helen was already sitting at their usual table with a mug and a stack of papers in front of her, along with what Elise knew was Helen's AA big book, the title concealed by the dust jacket from a copy of *Lucky* by Jackie Collins. Elise had seen the book on Helen's lap at a meeting once in her very early sobriety, and when Helen opened it and started reading "How It Works," out loud to open the meeting, Elise decided that she'd ask Helen to be her sponsor.

Helen didn't waste any time. As soon as Elise was settled with her own cup of coffee, she slid the papers, a stack of identical worksheets labeled "Step Nine," in front of Elise and smiled.

"Big day, buddy. Step Nine. Did you ask your Higher Power to help you become willing to make your amends?"

Elise shifted in her seat. "I asked for the willingness to be willing," she answered. "Good enough?" She looked down at the columns on the page in front of her, with spaces to write the name of the person to whom she owed an amends and the details of the harm she'd caused. The bottom half of the page was blank, with space to plan out exactly what she'd say, being careful to avoid mentioning anything except her part in things.

"We'll see," Helen answered.

Helen was only a few years older than Elise but seemed so much more together. Every time Elise saw her, Helen was wearing crisp, black-and-white separates that fit her perfectly, accessorized with tasteful silver jewelry and pointy-toed, black flats. Helen had a job as a paralegal that she didn't hate. She was single on purpose: a fact of Helen's life that was at once admirable and unsettling to Elise. She couldn't help but think that Helen was wasting some premium H-O-T-T *hot* years but didn't dare say that to her. After all, Helen was the one who'd taught her that "what other people think of us is none of our business."

Elise stacked the worksheets together and folded them in half. "Listen, I'm totally up for doing this, but I think I'm already at Step Ten. And Eleven. And in a way? Twelve?"

Helen nodded, unfolding the worksheets, and took a pen from her purse. "I know it feels like things start to happen quickly and you're getting some relief, but it is best to work all the steps in order. So many people stop after the third step, thinking they are really surrendering. They don't even know how good it can get." She pushed the papers toward Elise and laid the pen on top. "Give it a chance."

Elise took the worksheets from Helen and slid them into her purse. "It's beyond surrender for me right now, though. I feel like my HP is coming for me, whether I want to surrender or not. She's always there. The spiritual awakening is underway, like twenty-four-seven. I'd actually like to maybe get some relief from *that*."

Helen tilted her head and set her gaze just beyond Elise's shoulder, an expression Elise had come to recognize; it was the face that Helen made right before she reminded Elise that she wasn't a therapist and wouldn't give her advice. "Look babe," she started, "I'm here to work the steps with you. These are all just suggestions, not advice."

*Here it comes*, Elise thought.

"I mean, I'm not a therapist by any means at all."

*Bingo.*

"But, you're right about one thing. You never have to go it alone again. Your Higher Power is always there for you."

*That's what I'm afraid of.*

"And I'm here for you. Okay? Call me tomorrow. Call me sooner if you want to take a drink. I know this part is hard, but you'll feel so much better when you start to clean up your side of the street." Helen took a final sip of her coffee and reached for Elise's hands. "Serenity Prayer?"

Elise nodded.

"God," Helen started.

"Grant me the serenity…" Elise joined in.

Elise made it to Thursday, six months of sobriety, and Helen gave her one of her old six-month chips at the meeting.

"I can have this? Are you sure?" Elise asked, turning the dark blue coin over in her hand.

"Oh, yeah, I have a few of those," Helen said, waving a hand in the direction of the chip. "It took a long time to put together one whole year of sobriety."

"More than a year?"

Helen laughed and squeezed Elise's forearm, "Yeah, friend. Like, I don't know? Three years? Keep coming back." She walked toward the double doors of the meeting room. "Hit that step work, too. Step Nine," she called over her shoulder.

Elise hit her step work. She took out the list of people she'd harmed in her addiction and decided she'd start with a softball, a person who'd forgiven her over and over again, who loved her no matter what and, she could tell, secretly admired some of her wild, awful choices: Carrie. The worksheet got on her nerves, so she turned it over and used the clean side to compose an amends letter to her sister. The main thing she wanted to clear up with Carrie had to do with her own coming out. Their mother was furious when Elise told her family she was queer. She took it personally, blaming their father for dying on them all and leaving the girls without a man to love, a man whose image they could project onto their future husbands. Then she blamed Carrie, saying that Elise was impressionable, imitating Carrie to earn her love. Carrie stayed away for an entire year, which broke their mother's heart even more than having not one but two daughters who'd never have a Catholic wedding and a whole slew of Catholic children, as many as God saw fit to give them. Elise and her queerness became background noise, a relief. She was enjoying herself, messily sleeping with a bunch of her co-workers and newly curious former sorority sisters, spending her whole paycheck at gay bars, doing X and dancing every weekend. Carrie and Elise patched things up eventually, but things were stiff between Carrie and their mother for a long time, and the subject was a sore one, still.

Elise finished the letter and read it out loud, then texted a picture of what she'd written to Helen. Elise texted Michael about her plans to make amends to Carrie and asked if she would pray for her.

Michael wrote back.

> Of course
> I pray for you every day.

> You do?

> Your name is on my
> gratitude list every single
> day.

> Ty.

Elise felt a pang of disappointment at Michael's response, knowing that Michael would be saying AA prayers for her and not some hardcore Catholic convent prayers, a novena or a couple of decades of the Sorrowful Mysteries. She supposed she could ask Michael to do that, but the idea made her feel shy. She hadn't said anything about the chapel or the lady to Michael, mostly because Michael was so shut down about her time in the convent and any sort of spiritual experiences outside the ones she'd had in AA. Michael wasn't going to help her scratch that itch at all. She closed her eyes and said a prayer of surrender to her Higher Power, imagining herself depositing the letter in her HP's cold, shaking hands. Bloody tears splashed onto the words and the doves returned, covering it all with their cooing and their gray and white feathers.

Elise made plans to have lunch with Carrie on a Monday, the day the salon was closed.

Carrie was sitting on her front porch steps petting Christopher when Elise drove up. "I don't have anything for us to eat for lunch, buddy," Carrie called, "just yogurt and cigarettes."

"That sounds perfect," Elise said. She patted her knees with both hands and Christopher walked over and leaned against her legs. She tickled his ribs and scratched behind his ears. "Hi choux-choux, hello Prince Christopher, hello biscuit face. I love you more than a biscuit." She kissed his nose.

"Don't get him riled, Elise, I just gave him his medicine," Carrie said.

"Is he sick?" Elise looked into the dog's eyes. "You look fine to me, boss. You ok?"

"His Prozac. He is a biscuit face, though." She smiled at Christopher.

"Oh, that's *right*," Elise put her hand out and Christopher lifted his paw to shake. "Good man. Get that serotonin. I take that stuff, too, you know it? Twenty milligrams every day. Her, too," she pointed at Carrie.

"Nope, I'm team Wellbutrin," Carrie said.

"Boooooo."

"It's helping me, I think. I feel like it's turning my lights on again."

"You do seem better," Elise said. She'd noticed that Carrie seemed less enraged when she talked about Kim or the details of their divorce. She'd told Elise that she apologized to Kim for taking Christopher from Whole Foods instead of calling her lawyer and insisting that they fight to have him live with her full-time. Carrie was moving on. Elise knew that she'd gone on three dates with a woman she met on Tinder who seemed really into her, an accountant who left flowers and packs of cigarettes and tins of the cinnamon Altoids that Carrie loved on her porch between their dates, all of which Carrie had described as "fancy and hot." When Elise asked if Carrie had slept with the woman yet, she'd answered that she had, describing the experience as "fancy, but not *that* hot. It's nothing serious."

"Look, I want to tell you something," Elise began, concentrating on scratching Christopher's neck. She felt shy all of a sudden.

"Alright," Carrie got up, took Christopher's lead from a basket on the porch, "let's walk and talk, okay? He needs a good walk." She clipped the lead onto Christopher's collar and scratched the dog's neck, too. She found Elise's fingers and squeezed. "Something wrong?"

"No, I don't think so."

As they followed Christopher up and down the streets of Carrie's new neighborhood near downtown Baton Rouge, stopping to let him sniff and pee, Elise read the amends she'd written to Carrie from the worksheet. She'd stored the folded paper in her bra since the dress she was wearing didn't have pockets, and her palms were sweaty from nerves, so the paper had gotten floppy and soggy.

"Carrie, I need to say this to you so that I can stay sober. I was wrong to let you take all that heat when I came out. I didn't defend you or speak up for myself at all. I was horrible to you. You didn't do anything wrong and your anger was completely appropriate."

Carrie pushed Elise's hand down. "Look at me, Elise," she said with a pained smile. "Put that down and talk to me like a person you know."

Elise started crying, "This is hard, and I just, I'm really sorry. I'm not supposed to say I'm sorry, though. I'm supposed to say that I was wrong and ask what I can do to make things right with you."

Carrie put her hand through the loop at the end of Christopher's lead and wrapped her arms around Elise.

"I was wrong," Elise said, sobbing into Carrie's neck. "What can I do to make it right?"

Carrie tightened her hold on Elise and swayed a little, side to side. "It's right now, baby. Don't think about it anymore. It's all alright."

"Are you sure?"

Carrie felt a lump forming in her throat, remembering that time in her life, and how shitty it had all made her feel. How shitty Elise and her mother had acted toward her, in different shitty ways.

Christopher moved into the space between them and leaned onto Carrie's legs. The tenderness in that gesture was almost unbearable, and it triggered her own tears. *Thanks, Biscuit,* she thought.

"Yes, Elise. I'm sure. Just don't do me that way again."

# XI

## ALL THE APPS AGAIN

After the Jamie thing, Jody downloaded all the apps again. Bumble and Hinge filled her with low-grade dread, and swiping on Tinder grossed her out, but she had to keep it moving. She'd met Jamie on Bumble and found it to be the least chaotic—her settings resulted in lots of profiles of okay-seeming women in their thirties and forties that identified as bi or queer or gay. She noticed that she matched with a lot of Tauruses, women who answered "Sometimes" to working out, drinking, and smoking pot. Some of the dates went fine. She'd felt sort of hopeful about a woman named Celeste who owned a bike shop near the university but she lost interest when Celeste texted her one Monday evening, asking if Jody wanted to hang out because she was bored.

"I don't resonate with boredom. What is that. Tell me what that means," she said to Oliver afterward. They'd taken a ride to New Orleans for the day to make up for the ruined plans with Jamie. Jody wore her ho pride tank top and cutoffs with Jordans and Oliver wore a t-shirt with a picture of Mike Tyson on it that said, Everybody Has a Plan Until They Get Punched in the Mouth.

"I got nothing for that, *chér*. I don't know this boredom.

Like damn, read a book." They went to the fancy paper shop and Jody got some linen and onionskin for cranes. Oliver bought some pink Depression glass at a shop on Royal to take home and smash for mosaics. They ate raw oysters and Oliver got hammered on draft beer, so Jody drove them home. She always got teary when she crossed Lake Pontchartrain.

She made herself take the dating apps seriously. Even Tinder. Oliver had helped her set up profiles for each one, and that one was spicy. "Send me some sexy pictures," he said, and she sent six: Three smiling, two no smile but big eyes, and one laughing. She wore jeans in three of them. In one, she held a blowtorch in her studio at the university. One was overalls. One was running shorts and a sweaty t-shirt.

She saw Elise on Tinder right away. The picture was one Jody had taken a year before on a trip they'd taken to Rosemary Beach. Elise wore a pink strapless bathing suit, her long blonde ponytail draped across one bare shoulder. A pair of sunglasses with red plastic frames rested on top of her head. In the background, sunlight shimmered over the Gulf of Mexico. Jody swiped left. *See ya never.* She wondered for a second if Michael knew and then pushed that thought away and kept going.

A dozen faces later, Elise's older sister Carrie appeared. She swiped right. They matched. Jody put her phone face down on the coffee table. *Fuckfuckfuck.* She walked around the living room and sat down on the couch again. She slid her hands under her thighs and looked over at the phone.

It dinged, but it was a text message, not a Tinder notification—her neighbor, asking her to check and see if he'd left the sprinkler on. She walked to the front door. He had.

Yeah, man I can turn that off if you need.

Thanks Jo I owe you one.

She walked around the side of the house and let herself into his back yard and turned off the faucet. When she got back, Carrie had sent her a message.

Well.

She shoved her phone in the back pocket of her shorts and walked into her own backyard and stood there with her hands over her mouth. She took a screenshot of the screen with their faces that said, *It's a Match!* and sent it to Oliver without comment.

Oh you still like mess huh?

I know???

Damn I remember her. She's scary.

I know.

Finer than a mfer tho.

I KNOW.

See!!! Fuhhhhhhh.

She sent a screenshot of Carrie's one-word message next. They had both met Carrie before, when Elise brought her sister to their sophomore year art exhibition. Jodie and Oliver were in printmaking then, and partners in a class on the lithograph. The image they'd made together was simple—a recreation of a photograph a cluster of Roseate Spoonbills bathing in a cypress grove at the edge of a swamp in St. Martin parish. They'd blown it up and used peach and fuchsia ink to print it on an old calico bedsheet and stretched the whole thing on a frame they'd constructed with wood they'd salvaged from a busted pirogue Oliver found at his dad's house. They made a B.

It was the first time Elise had brought her family around. She was proud of Jody and they were just falling in love, so everything felt complicated in an exciting way. Oliver was right: Carrie scared them. Elise waited at the gallery door and when Carrie walked in Jody remembered how alike they looked; Elise kept framed photos of herself with Carrie and Teddie, their older sister, in their living room, plus a few snapshots stuck to their fridge with magnets. Same long ash-blonde hair, same brown eyes. Carrie was a little taller than Elise, maybe 5'5, and heavier, but the real difference was in the way she moved. She didn't walk into a room so much as she glided in. Like an empress. Jody automatically assumed Carrie was stuck on herself, and she wasn't exactly wrong.

When Jody approached them and stuck out her hand, Carrie slid her sunglasses on top of her head and crossed her arms.

"Carrie. Pleasure," she nodded at Jody's hand, "I don't do that. Where's your painting?"

She wore a white linen sheath with sandals. Gold hoops and bracelets, same as Elise. She held her handbag, slouchy and made of camel-colored leather, in the crook of her arm. Jody could smell Carrie's perfume, something smoky mixed with spice.

"Oh, it's actually a lithograph."

"Alright, then. Where is that? Where is your lithograph?"

Jody walked Carrie over to the piece, and Elise followed. She explained the process of taking the photo and printing it, and when she started talking about the frame, Oliver walked up and introduced himself to Carrie, who looked at him hard for a few seconds and turned back to the lithograph.

"Why don't I take you all out for drinks. When is this," she waved her hand in the direction of the rest of the pieces and the table loaded with depressing veggie trays and tubs of hummus in the corner, "over?"

Elise looked at Jody and Jody looked at Oliver, who looked at the ground.

"Somebody answer me," Carrie said after a beat.

"Now," Oliver answered. "We can go now."

They walked from the art building to a bar just off campus

that Elise and Jody knew about. When they walked in, "Hold Me" by Fleetwood Mac was playing in the dim space and Carrie turned to Elise, "This song is never not playing in here. Put something else on, please." She gave Elise a handful of change from her wallet for the jukebox. "Fleetwood Mac is for putting a scarf over a lamp and drinking alone in your bedroom."

Jody remembered the questions Carrie had asked her that night, all pretty standard, are-you-good-enough-for-my-sister inquiries. Over the course of an hour or so she asked:

- Where Jody was from (Biloxi).
- How many siblings she had (three).
- If she was close to them (not really).
- When she was graduating (two years).
- What she planned to do with a degree in studio art (no idea).
- When her birthday was (October).
- If she was a Libra or Scorpio (cusp).
- How old she was (thirty-four).
- How long she'd lived in Baton Rouge (five years).

Elise and Oliver played "Lucky Ones" by Lana Del Rey and a bunch of songs by the Sugarcubes and a few by just Björk on the jukebox and talked to each other. Jody saw Oliver looking at Carrie a couple of times, and he finally mustered the courage to ask her some questions, too.

"Didn't you go to LSU?"

She turned in her chair to face him and re-crossed her legs. "Yes. I majored in Comm."

"When was that?"

Elise leveled her eyes at Jody, as if to say, *buckle up*. "Are you asking how old I am?"

"No, I just—"

"How old do you think I am?"

Oliver underestimated Carrie and tried to play with her a little bit. "How old do you think I am?"

"I think you're twenty-nine. You know what they say," she took a sip of the glass of white wine she'd ordered, "if a man hasn't made it by the time he's thirty, he'll never make it."

Oliver wasn't smiling anymore, "Hell on that. What is *make* it? Who is *they*?"

Carrie set her glass down. "How old *are* you?"

"Twenty-nine."

The mood was chilly until everyone had another round of drinks, and Oliver offered to walk Carrie to her car when she said she was ready to go. He later told Jody that he'd put his hand on Carrie's waist and tried to open her car door.

"She swatted me and said, 'Son, don't bother, I'm a lesbian.' She called me *son*."

"That is beautiful. You deserved that takedown."

"Tell Elise I want her number."

"Hell, no. You heard what she said."

"That's real?"

"Yes, why would she lie? Never mind."

Jody typed and re-typed responses to Carrie's message.

This isn't awkward at all.

You look amazing!

How have you been?

Coffee soon?

Can I take you to dinner?

When can I take you to dinner?

They all felt artificial and forced. Should she just type "Well" back? She agonized over it for another minute. She wrote:

> Well. This isn't awkward at all. You look amazing. When can I take you to dinner?

Her finger hovered over the send icon. She sent it.

Carrie responded thirty minutes later.

> Why don't you come by mine for a drink tomorrow evening. We can catch up. Five?

The next morning, Jody decided to ride her bike to her studio. The weather wouldn't be cool much longer and she was too excited about whatever she was doing with Carrie that evening. Was it a date? "I Drove All Night" by Roy Orbison was on when she reached the north gate of campus, and when she looked down to turn up the music in her headphones, her front tire grazed a curb and she fell off her bike. One minute Roy Orbison was singing, "Is that alright?" and the next, she was flat on her ass in the neutral ground. When she stood up, lightning shot down her leg. Her tailbone was on fire. She picked up her bike and started walking it to the art building, but she had to stop and sit down, and that felt impossible. *Tailbone. On fire.* When she tried to stand, her lower back erupted in a spasm that took her breath away. She texted Oliver.

His response:

> Mama I'm at Grand Isle with my "parents," puh! Come get ME.

Kelly was with him.

She could call an Uber, she supposed. The idea of that filled her with self-pity, though, and she started crying. She wanted someone to come and get her who would know what to do. She wanted Carrie to come and get her.

> Hey. Are you busy? I need a favor.

Carrie wrapped a couple of bags of frozen vegetables in a dishtowel and secured the whole thing with a rubber band and drove over to campus to get Jody. She laid the passenger seat in her BMW flat and helped Jody into the car, then walked Jody's bike the rest of the way to her studio and locked it up inside.

"What do you need? Advil?"

"Yeah," Jody winced as Carrie braked at a light.

"Epsom salts? Maybe a real ice pack?"

"Yeah," Jody shifted onto her side.

"Whiskey?"

"I don't do that anymore."

"Oh no? Weren't we going to have drinks tonight?"

"I just don't drink booze anymore. I quit when Elise quit."

"Oh." Carrie looked straight ahead as she drove toward the house Jody had shared with her sister. "So you're not an alcoholic? I'm confused."

"No, I just wanted to be there for her. I wanted to help," Jody answered.

"Right, so you need Al-Anon. That's textbook codependent behavior."

"I go to Al-Anon, too. That's where I met—"

"Michael. That's right," Carrie said. "I did know that, never mind."

"Yeah," Jody adjusted the frozen vegetables. "Michael."

Carrie reached over and adjusted Jody's seatbelt into place. "Do you have anything to help with this at your house?"

"No."

"I do."

Jody sighed, relieved, "Can we—"

"I guess we better." Carrie took a left at the stoplight and then another left and a right. She took Jody to her house.

Jody limped inside and laid on the couch while Carrie made glasses of chocolate milk for the two of them. She rummaged around in her medicine cabinet until she found a bottle of Advil, a bottle of Tylenol, and a couple of leftover Percocet from a root canal she'd had the year before. She brought all three bottles to Jody. "Okay, so, greatest hits," she shook the bottles of Advil and Tylenol, "or these bad boys?" She held up the prescription bottle.

"Those bad boys."

"Right. I think I'll have one, too." She shook one of the pills into her hand and sat down at the end of the couch and passed Jody the bottle and a glass of chocolate milk. "Poor you. Are you comfortable?"

"I'm okay," Jody laughed. "Are you about to get high right now?"

"Just a little. Is that okay?"

Jody took a Percocet and a couple of Advil with a swallow of chocolate milk. She reached for the remote control lying on the coffee table in front of her. "What channels do you have?"

"Every channel."

"Good, there's a documentary about Hilma af Klint I want to watch."

"Oh, I know about that," Carrie held her hand out for the remote. "Give it here."

Carrie found the film and started it. She got up to close the blinds, and then walked to the linen closet in the hall near her bedroom. "Do you want a blanket?" She called. "I like to keep the AC on snowballs." She took a cotton blanket and a pillow to the living room. "Under your knees?" She held up the pillow and Jody moved her legs to make space. Sliding it under Jody's knees, Carrie brushed some grass and dirt from the couch cushions, "Don't come back here until you can sit on my couch right," she joked. "Can't believe I'm letting you put your feet on my nice Nancy Meyers movie couch. Damn."

"Sorry, dude. I picked up some of the neutral ground when I crashed," Jody said. "Which Nancy Meyers movie?"

"All of them?" She sat on the couch and Jody stretched her legs until her feet were in Carrie's lap. "I decided I wanted my divorcée experience to be pure Nancy Meyers fantasy. White furniture. White kitchen. White jeans, cashmere t-shirts," she gestured at her outfit: white jeans and a pale-yellow cashmere t-shirt.

"White wine. Bouncy hair. Don't-need-nobody type of attitude?" Jody chimed in.

Carrie laughed, "That's right. She's got a lot of errands to run. She's got a lot of crying to do."

"You're nailing it."

"I know." Carrie realized she'd been absentmindedly squeezing Jody's ankle. She patted it. "Sorry." She looked at the television. "Should I start this over?"

"Yeah, but don't stop."

Carrie put her hands on Jody's ankle and left them there. When the film was over, Jody asked if she could stay a little longer. "I'm not ready to go home just yet." She sat up and stretched her back. She reached for Carrie's hands and kissed them, one at a time.

"You can stay here as long as you want."

They were together after that. Jody slept at Carrie's house that night and never really left, except to go to her own house for a couple of nights, and Carrie came with her then. They both wanted to be at Carrie's bigger, nicer place all the time, but there was Elise to consider. They were dodging Elise. Jody knew Elise had been staying with Carrie some, and that she didn't really have a place of her own. Carrie kept Elise at bay for a couple of nights by telling Elise she had a stomach bug.

One evening a couple of weeks in, she and Jody stood in her kitchen and tried to talk about a way to tell Elise what was happening.

"I say we tell her nothing. Just let her find out." Jody was annoyed at having to think about Elise at all. She was into Carrie and she wanted to only think about that. Because of her cranky back, they'd almost had sex three or four times before they were finally able to do it, and that waiting had made her crazy in a way she liked. They both liked it. They had kissed until they were weak and put their hands all over each other. Looked at each other for as long as they wanted. Jody watched Carrie fix her hair in the morning, watched her while she cooked and watered her lawn. She had seen the way that Carrie rubbed lotion on her hands throughout the day, and thought that it was sexy in a way that was different from the sexy way she rubbed lotion on the rest of her body after she took a bath. She felt Carrie looking at her all the time, too.

She caught herself comparing Carrie to Elise every day. They hadn't been around each other much when she and Elise were together, and now she could see that some of their similarities extended beyond the way they looked. The differences between Carrie and Elise were what attracted her, though. One afternoon she'd snuck a look at the cabinet in Carrie's kitchen where she kept her medicine and vitamins. The bottle of leftover Percocet was there. She picked up the bottle and looked at the date: a year had passed since Carrie had filled the prescription and at least ten of the twenty prescribed pills were there. She put the bottle back where she found it and went into the living room where Carrie was lying on the couch, looking out the window at a hummingbird hovering over the feeder she'd hung on the patio, and she laid on the couch next to Carrie and kissed her for a long, long time.

Jody was smashing a half dozen Lenox Christmas plates in a pillowcase with a hammer for a project at her house one afternoon when Carrie called to ask her for a few hours alone that night at her house with Elise. "I'm going to go ahead and tell her. She wants me to watch *Agnes of God* with her again. I think she's still on the religious thing. Have you ever seen that movie?'

"Yeah, with her. Really upsetting."

"Truly. When the blood sort of squirts out of her palms? That's not really how I picture stigmata, but—"

"So, you're ready to have that talk with her?"

"I need to. Ducking her is getting old, no? It's going to be so bad, but it'll be out there. She made that amends to me. I should do that. Right?"

"You better talk to your sponsor about that first. Don't just charge in with an amends before you talk to her."

"Right," Carrie tapped her chin with her index finger. "I'll call Julie."

"Who's that?"

"My sponsor," Carrie answered.

JudgeJulie is your sponsor too?

Yeah. Why? Yours?

Jody raised her eyebrows and opened her mouth to say something, then closed it.

"Fucking anonymity," Carrie said.

Jody walked over and took Carrie's hands. "Look, maybe Elise won't care," Jody said. "I don't think she cares about what I do at all."

"She cares about what I do."

Jody soothed Carrie a little and said she'd come over whenever she wanted, or stay away for awhile. "Do you want closeness or space?"

"Closeness. I'm probably going to need some tlc."

"You can have whatever you want."

"Whatever I want?"

"I will absolutely wear you out when I see you," Jody laughed.

"Okay but I might want you to bring me a pack of cigarettes, too. *Agnes of God* is going to make me want to smoke. Two straight hours of smoking. Even the nuns."

# XII

## BACK IN THE CUP

Elise knew everything. Even before Carrie called, she knew what her sister and Jody had been up to. Michael told her. She'd seen them get into Carrie's car together after a noon meeting.

"So? They know each other," Elise said.

Michael had seen them kiss too. She'd watched them kissing for a good while before Carrie started the car and drove away.

"Look at me," Elise said, when Michael finished talking.

But Michael wouldn't look up. She sat at the kitchen table, staring at her hands.

Elise pushed herself off Michael's bed and walked around the apartment, lapping the table and wandering back into and out of the kitchen. Suddenly Elise felt giddy and astonished, and full of a cold wired energy she didn't particularly like. In that moment, Elise knew everything: that Michael wouldn't look at her because she still loved Jody, and that she and Michael were done. She found her sandals and car keys and cigarettes and left.

She drove around for hours with the radio on. She couldn't stand to hear music so she set the dial to NPR. Smoked a bunch of cigarettes. Pulled into the Popeye's parking lot, back behind the package store, to breathe and make her plan. She would drive back to her sister's and tell Carrie she knew all about her.

Nothing Carrie would say could make this right. She would show up at Jody's work and break a glass or two and leave a nasty note on her car. She would go back home and seduce Michael and make their relationship work the way it should. Nothing felt right. She would get wasted on something, on everything, and all her go-to, substitute substances—rage and desire and nicotine—would not penetrate her pain. If Michael loved Jody, and Jody loved Carrie, and Carrie loved Jody, who the fuck would be left to love her? She was on her knees.

She would get out of the car. Across the lot to the package store. . . . She was on her knees in the Popeye's parking lot. Then she was sitting on her hands in the parking lot of Our Lady, Star-of-the-Sea. When it was time to go she heard her mother's voice: "Put it in the cup."

Summoning the facts of her life, she imagined a version of the surrender Helen kept pushing her to make, a vision of herself in a soaking-wet robe, her feet transformed into roses. Her hands clasped in front of her chest, and she felt a pulsing energy there. Through the spaces her fingers made, she glimpsed something grayish-white and alive. She imagined Michael. Her life with Michael: into the cup. Her relationship with Jody: into the cup. Jody and Michael and Jody and Carrie: into the cup.

Jeanne hovered at the foot of the altar, holding the chalice. After each person sipped, she wiped it precisely with a crisp white cloth, then handed the cup to the next person.

Elise took the host from the priest who'd said Mass and held it on her tongue, letting it soften enough to swallow. Back in catechism, she'd learned to do this, to never touch the body of Christ with her hands or her teeth. Since she'd been sober, she'd only ever tilted the chalice gently, allowing the wine to barely touch her upper lip.

When she reached Jeanne she took the chalice in both hands, freeing the doves she'd been holding. She lifted it to her lips and took a strong pull, head back, making space for her life in the chalice's golden bowl.

She held the wine in her mouth—for a beat—letting her tongue absorb some of its sweetness, and then she let it all flow back into the cup.

# ACKNOWLEDGMENTS

I have immense gratitude and love for Megan Clark and Rodney Wilhite, whose presence, friendship, humor, and care have seen me through some *times*. I thank my lucky stars for those two.

These friends and colleagues have sustained me with their support, too: Nichola Torbett, Davis McCombs & Carolyn Guinzio, Toni Jensen, Geffrey Davis, Padma Viswanathan, Geoff Brock, Bryan Hurt, Rebecca Gayle Howell, Lindsey Aloia, Gwynne Gertz, Carol Guess, Katie Nichol, and Kathy McGregor. None of this would be any fun without you all. Thank you for being there—it means so much to me.

Big-time appreciations go to the editors *Bayou Magazine, Feels Blind Literary Magazine, Apple in the Dark,* and *Cream City Review.* Versions of "Anger Prayer," "Hand to Mouth," "The Apartment Song," and "Cardio Annihilation" appeared as stories in their pages, and it was a joy to be included. Thanks so much for taking good care of my work.

Gratitude to Lacy M. Johnson, Canese Jarboe, Lindsay Klarc Chudzik, and Rachel Kincaid for guidance and kind words.

Thanks to Texas Review Press for accompanying this work into the world. Special thanks go to my editor PJ Carlisle, who helped make the story sing.

Tremendous gratitude to Renee Gladman, who chose this work for the 2022 Clay Reynolds Novella Prize, an honor I'm still over-the-moon excited to have received.

Massive thanks are due to my mother, who is basically a saint.